Spanish Journals

The Posthumous Diary of an Expat

PART THREE - CONSOLIDATION

A R Lowe

A R Lowe ©2013

The right of A R Lowe to be identified as the author of this work has been asserted by him in accordance with the Copyright, Design and Patents Act 1988.

This diary is a work of fiction. All names, characters and events are the product of the author's imagination and any resemblance to actual events or to persons, living or dead, is entirely coincidental.

ISBN-13: 978-1494275945
ISBN-10: 1494275945

Introduction by Pamela Postlethwaite

As I put pen to paper to write the introduction to the third instalment of my late husband's diary*, I can but feel grateful to him that public demand for his increasingly eloquent scribblings has exceeded everyone's expectations except his own and that it does indeed appear that, as he once said:

"People need to know that a nondescript commuter like me can carve out a new life for himself and his wife in the rugged terrain of inland Spain. I shall prove that one is never too old to embrace a simpler, more natural, and more productive lifestyle and integrate into this rustic community. I will not succumb to the temptations of an aimless expat existence!"

I do not mean to suggest that I remember this little speech word for word or, indeed, that he said it all at once, but he said so many things of this nature and said them so often that it would be almost impossible to misquote him. He once called me, rather absurdly I thought at the time, a 'Doubting Pamela', and, as I look out from my new conservatory over the pool to the sparkling sea where his ashes were finally scattered, I wipe away tears of fond remembrance for my late husband Ernest and thank him sincerely that in the end we both achieved the lifestyle that we aspired to, although no amount of leisurely living could ever compensate for the loss of my singular spouse.

During the time that this part of the diary recounts, Ernest hoped to consolidate what he called his 'non-expat status' and complete the integration process which he was thoroughly convinced that he was well on the way to achieving. I leave it to the gracious reading public to decide to what extent he realised this noble ambition and hope that they enjoy his account of these unexpectedly turbulent months.

Pamela Postlethwaite,
Javea,
Spain
December 2013

* which includes all Ernest's additional annotations (in parenthesis). Words which he underlined have been italicised.

PART THREE - CONSOLIDATION

Lunes, 1 de SEPTIEMBRE 2008

What better way to start my first ever September in Spain than by removing the cellophane from a brand new journal and writing my first tentative words with the splendidly engraved fountain pen which Paco and Laura presented to me for my fifty-fifth birthday, celebrated with much 'festejo' (festivity) only three days ago. The level of acceptance which I have attained in that section of our little community - Paco, Laura and, I assume, their teenage son Paco - manifests itself in the fact that in their eyes I am no longer Ernest, but *Ernesto* Postlethwaite! From now on I will encourage the use of the Spanish version of my name and thus blend in even more with the other village men; something that my stoical summer-long trouser wearing must have already gone some way to achieving, despite the severe, sweaty discomfort which it has caused me. I am looking forward to the cooler weather which, while a soothing relief to productive agricultural workers such as myself, must be a disappointment to the sun-dried expat layabouts.

Lena and Gerald, who delighted me by their surprise arrival on my birthday, will be with us for another week, prior to visiting Lena's parents in Germany to obtain their blessing for Gerald to whisk her off to a godforsaken antipodean commune for a year. They appear to be pushing the date of departure to Australia back and I, by means of subtle reasoning and cunning persuasion, intend to push it back to the end of time, as I would much rather they stayed in Europe, preferably in Spain, prior to occupying Nora and Angeles's house when that pair of rustics shuffle off their mortal coils at some point in the next ten, or even five, years.

But, as Pamela says, Gerald must first bow down to Mammon and prove himself capable of earning his crust like the rest of us, as she will not allow me and the sausage purveyor to simply buy them the house. Hopefully their trip to meet his future parents-in-law will fertilize the seed of conformity which Pamela planted in his unconventional brain during their last visit, and the Bavarian air will throw up some ideas acceptable to his shockingly idealistic temperament. I also hope that he will cut his hair before he goes and rid himself of that appalling ponytail. Germans have always favoured short hair, I believe, but I fear that the crew cut which might ingratiate him with the ham baron will not be forthcoming. I will speak to Pamela about the hair issue as her persuasive powers are unparalleled. (First alliteration with my new pen.) While she is at it, she might as well also address the dress issue, as I am sure that multi-coloured waistcoats are not standard attire in Germany and may even be banned. Ya veremos. (For the uninitiated: We will see.)

I must, however, tread carefully as this week I require Gerald's assistance with the construction of a goat pen for

Ernestina and her future offspring. My research on the internet has yet to reveal a flat pack option and my construction skills, although improving, are still inadequate for an undertaking of such magnitude. I also need him to advise me on what is to be done with all the plants on the plot when they have ceased to produce edible growth. Do I, for instance, prune the tomato and pepper plants? I don't know, but I hope to find out without showing myself to be overly ignorant and thus diminishing my powers of persuasion in more crucial - monetary, geographical and hairdressing - matters.

As I wipe my nib for the umpteenth time, it occurs to me that an amalgamation of my son and myself would produce a being supremely equipped to confront the challenges of the modern world. If I can add his manual skills to my administrative, financial, organisational, deductive, and, dare I say it, linguistic abilities, I will consider myself a thoroughly well-rounded person. Ditto for Gerald if he gets a proper job.

Martes, 2 de Septiembre (or 'Setiembre' - odd.)

Today has been a most satisfactory day, my contentment commencing at breakfast when Gerald and Lena declared that we might dispense with the trip to the seaside to see our neighbours Rocío and Pedro perform for the foreigners, as their impromptu concert at my birthday party was quite enough Flamenco music for one week. I acquiesced happily to omitting this visit to the expat-infested coast as, although our last excursion was pleasant enough, I feel I have used up the quota of unproductive beach outings that a humble peasant farmer can permit himself in one year. I promised to take them to see our illustrious neighbours perform at one of their totally non-guiri concerts during the winter.

"We'll be in Australia," said Gerald.

"Oh, of course," I replied, smiling at Gerald and, when he wasn't looking, catching Lena's eye and sighing sadly. The fruits of my Australian internet research should be ready to put into effect tomorrow.

After our Spanish breakfast of toast and jam with café con leche - it just comes out in Spanish now before I can stop my pen - I steered Gerald outside and said that Ernestina looked rather dejected, tied as she was to the fence and half way through chewing her fifth length of rope. By way of reply he produced a sheet of paper from his waistcoat pocket on which he had sketched out a design for the goat pen with sleeping quarters included! I should never underestimate my resourceful and thoughtful, if slightly misguided, son and I took the paper enthusiastically and paced about the plot looking for the ideal spot on which to build this latest addition to my mini-farm. I gazed wistfully over the fence at Rocío and Pedro's scrapyard which I hope to make my own - minus the rusting cars - at some point in the not too distant future, and even more longingly at Nora and Angeles's well-tended allotment and orchard which will need little improvement save ripping down the fence when they are no longer with us.

After apologising to Sancho for his unusually short walk, Gerald and I drove into Villeda to the carpintería and the builders' merchant's - 'suministros de construcción' - not 'construccionaría' as I had mistakenly guessed - and bought all the timber, fencing, sand, cement, gravel and other sundry items which we require for our project. *All* of these materials fit into and on top of my huge, practical car, including a fine farm-style gate which, although rather expensive, will add a professional touch to my caprine (goaty) haven, while a shiny green wheelbarrow put the finishing touch to my loaded roof rack. When I asked the portly, weather - or drink - beaten builders' merchant if he preferred cash or card, he declared that 'efectivo' (Effective money? As opposed to ineffective money?) was 'mucho mucho mejor' (much much better), leading me to suspect that a proportion of his taxable income goes straight into his stomach, but no matter.

After steering my overburdened workhorse home and changing Ernestina's rope for what I hope will be the last time, Gerald instructed me how to mix concrete in the wheelbarrow while he set to digging the holes for the fence posts. While slaving away with my spade, I *felt* the presence of Nora observing me over the fence and his cry of, "No, no, no, no!" was most unwelcome, if not unexpected, as he only addresses me verbally when he feels I am in error. His wrinkly head disappeared and before I had wiped the sweat from my brow he appeared behind me wielding his azada (big hoe), before plunging it into the mixture and heaving it to and fro to surprisingly good effect. I allowed him to mix a barrowful and wheel it over to the first post hole, before excusing myself to go to the bathroom. I watched him mixing a second barrowful from the kitchen window until Pamela shooed me outside, saying that I should be ashamed of myself and that the poor old man would strain his heart.

Leaving a witty retort wisely unsaid, I went out, relieved him of his tool, and mixed a load under his careful and most annoying supervision. His instructive miming was so vigorous that he might as well have done the job himself and it was only the sight of Pamela, arms crossed, at the kitchen window which prevented me from returning the azada to his gnarled hands and taking Sancho for a proper walk.

My blistered hands have made my writing so clumsy that I have resorted to a ballpoint to finish today's journal entry. By the end of the afternoon all the fence posts were in place and tomorrow we will attach the metal mesh and put up the handsome gate, prior to releasing Ernestina into her new domain.

Miércoles, 3 de Septiembre

After another backbreaking day's work, the goat pen is now fully erect and this afternoon we began to construct the framework for Ernestina's abode. She watched us so attentively that I am sure she realised that she was to be the future tenant and when I released her into the pen for the first time she settled down within the timbers of her new house. Sancho sniffed around the perimeter, glancing at me reproachfully from time to time, until I pointed out that he already had a home and a very comfortable one at that. Tomorrow I will take him for at least one proper walk.

Today has been doubly gratifying as Lena's reaction to the photographs which I printed out and showed to her in Gerald's absence exceeded all my expectations. As I explained the murderous qualities of the deadly taipan snake, the red back and funnel web spiders, and, mindful of her love of the sea, the lethal box jellyfish, her lovely blue eyes widened in alarm and she said that Gerald, when describing the delights of the cuddly koala, the playful possum and the cute little bandicoot, had omitted to mention these less appealing creatures. I urged her not to mention this revelation to Gerald as he might mistakenly believe that I was against them going 'down under', but I felt it my obligation to avail her of the lethal qualities of some of the fauna, especially as they would be living in the middle of nowhere, miles from the nearest hospital. I expect the effects of our little chat to manifest themselves within the next forty-eight hours.

Pamela has seen the funny side of my crafty exploitation of Nora and said that it brought to mind the fence painting scene in Tom Sawyer. I believe that we have that book in our humble library, so I will take it to bed with me and see for myself.

Jueves, 4 de Septiembre

As Lena wished to accompany me on Sancho's walk this morning, I chose a route through the village in order to share her beauty with the locals once more. It is a pity that she is not Spanish, but the beautiful Spanish girls I have seen, mostly on television, do not look very practical. Lena *looks* practical, but her approach to life is less 'hands on' than I would wish and she is yet to make a significant contribution to the life of Integración, such as cooking a meal or - lest the future reader suspect me of sexism - sawing a plank.

Plank sawing was my allotted task this morning while Gerald screwed them to the structure tirelessly. His strength and stamina is astounding and he is indeed living proof that meat eating, while pleasant, is unnecessary. For the duration of their stay I will only resort to my corned beef supplies in the event of overwhelming withdrawal symptoms. While sawing I kept one eye on Nora's plot and, when his nut brown head finally appeared, I made a few clumsy cuts before taking off my glove, shaking my hand, and wincing in my most convincing manner. Sure enough, his head disappeared and before I had picked up the saw he came shuffling through the house - without knocking, of course - took up the tool, and set to work vigorously, smiling and nodding at me while I stroked my chin in thoughtful wonder at his mastery. When, four planks later, Pamela appeared at the back door, I took over proceedings until, on hearing the front door shut, my sawing went to pieces once more. Her bakery outing enabled Nora to get through twelve more planks before the clunk signalling her return spurred me into action with a notably improved technique which Nora, nodding like a madman, no doubt put down to his thorough demonstration. My adaptation of Tom Sawyer's whitewashing ploy kept my spirits up for the rest of the day and all that now remains is to put on the roof to make Casa Ernestina complete.

This evening while Lena and my son were walking Sancho, I approached Pamela regarding her potential contribution to my campaign to produce a more German-friendly Gerald. She harbours the delusion that Germany is one of the most progressive countries in Europe and accused me of 'history induced racism'. I conceded that it was true that it had now been a while since the last war, but that their sense of order, efficiency, and blind obedience is surely still prevalent in the business community, adding that I was anxious for Gerald to make as good an impression on Herr Krankl, Lena's father, as possible. She refused point blank to help me in this matter and reminded me of Gerald's considerable ability to win people over, even suggesting that cutting his hair might reduce his powers in this respect. I must admit that I cannot imagine him with short hair and I may have to concentrate my efforts on sartorial improvements.

I have started Tom Sawyer from the beginning to see if I can pick up any more tips from the rascally youth - youths, in fact, for Huck Finn is another wily creation of Twain's great brain.

Viernes, 5 de Septiembre

Anxious to conserve some energy for our visit to the 'Moros y Cristianos' fiesta in Villeda this evening, I got up ten minutes later than usual and worked conservatively on the goat house, which we completed by four o'clock. Ernestina, after sleeping within its wall when it was roofless, now refuses to enter the completed dwelling under any circumstances. I squeezed myself inside in order to remove any fears she might have regarding its sturdiness and it was whilst crouching therein that I had another of my brainwaves. A shed! I must have a shed and for the life of me do not know how I have managed without one until now. The covered porch area is cluttered with implements and I rushed inside to find Pamela and ask her if this untidy build-up of paraphernalia was not an eyesore.

"You've finally thought of a shed, then?" she said, before adding that I was *not* to induce Gerald to begin to build one of those too, as she had hardly spent any time with him and they would be leaving after the weekend. I protested that I had no such intention and that, after learning how to build a goat house, a slightly bigger structure should be well within my capabilities. My son, however, was of a different opinion, pointing out that a shed must have foundations and that after I had constructed those - following detailed instructions which he would write down for me - the best option would be to have a ready-made shed delivered and placed upon them, which would require pulling down some of the fence at the bottom of the plot to allow access. "But my crops!" I protested, to which he replied, "You'll be clearing those soon and digging it all over, won't you?" which conveniently settled that niggling doubt in my mind.

It is now seven o'clock and time to go and see how the townspeople re-enact the Moors versus Christians conflicts of old, which I will faithfully report on these pages tomorrow.

Sábado, 6 de Septiembre

Re-enactment is not exactly the word I would use to describe last night's proceedings, as what we witnessed was, in fact, 'La Entrada'; presumably the entrance of the two armies onto the field of battle, in this case by way of Villeda high street.

After parking my trusty vehicle on the edge of town, we followed the swarms of visitors into the centre and, all the café tables being full, stood huddled on the pavement awaiting the arrival of the first contingent of Christians. As the sound of martial brass band music grew louder, anticipation increased and before long a squadron of individuals came into view led by a splendidly attired bearded man who elicited applause from the crowd by waving a big sword around. His men, about twenty in number and all wearing very ornate helmets, marched solemnly to the beat of the drum, bobbing from side to side most pleasingly. As they drew alongside, my eye for historical detail was disappointed to see several of them smoking big cigars and at least two wearing wristwatches. Nor did I feel that the brass band which followed them and whose fat little drummer boy I recognised from the Easter processions could be an entirely authentic reproduction of any musical ensemble which may or may not have accompanied the Christian warriors into battle at least six hundred years ago, at which time I very much doubt that the trombone had been invented.

On expressing these misgivings to Pamela, she told me to shut up and enjoy the show, but for a man recently immersed in historical studies of the period, these discrepancies played on my mind; that and the fact that more than one of the 'soldiers' appeared to be tipsy. When the band had passed us by, I asked Lena and Gerald what they thought of it all. Lena said that she wasn't keen on anything warlike, which is understandable, but that the costumes were very nice, while Gerald said that it was, and I quote, 'a load of bollocks' and just an excuse for the exploiters and the exploited of the capitalist system to get together and justify their materialistic existence by showing off. Pamela said we were all killjoys and that she was off to get a drink, so it appeared that we were staying.

When the second 'comparsa' - for that is what each group is called - appeared, headed by another bearded, sword-wielding man, I had a distinct feeling of déjà vu and remembered the Easter processions which at least we had been able to endure from a comfortably seated position. My suggestion of an adjournment to a café until the Moors made their appearance was well received and after two small glasses of beer I felt sufficiently refreshed to await their arrival in a less critical and purist state of mind.

The Moors swayed rather than bobbed to slightly more oriental brass band music and their costumes and helmets were even more elaborate than those of the Christians, but other than that, proceedings were much the same. I was diverting myself by counting cigars, wristwatches and pairs of spectacles when I was surprised to see a row of women in one of the groups. One does not need to have read the Koran, which I haven't, to know that Muslim ladies were hardly likely to have gone into battle, especially not wearing visor-less silver helmets and makeup. Pamela and Lena applauded the women enthusiastically and I suppose it is true that they have as much right as anybody to take part in a pantomime of this kind.

The second to last group had blackened faces and, perhaps because they felt more camouflaged, were the most heretical - the members of the third row passing a brandy flask from hand to hand - and it was only the last group of Moors, called the 'Capitanía', which evoked any sense of authenticity. Their leader was on horseback and made his steed rear impressively as he brandished his enormous Moorish sword, while none of his men smoked, drank, wore spectacles, or could have told you the time. I will try to conserve the solemnity of this last group in my memory in case I am ever asked my opinion of the Moros y Cristianos fiesta by an aficionado of this type of extravaganza. I was surprised not to see my golf partner Alfredo taking part, keen as he is on the Easter processions, unless he was one of the face-blackened drunkards. I will ask him his opinion of this festival when Gerald and Lena's departure allows me to play golf once more.

Over breakfast today we compared mental notes on the fiesta. Gerald's were scarcely printable, while Pamela said that it was a pity that we didn't do things like that in Britain any more as it was celebrations of this kind that maintained a cohesive society; fine words for half past eight in the morning. Gerald scoffed, Lena scoffed her toast, but I did agree that she had a point and that the social decay prevalent in our former country, where most families spent more time goggling at the television than interacting with their fellow citizens, may well be down to the absence of such unifying activities. Pamela went on to say that if I was so keen to integrate, these fiestas were exactly the kind of thing I should be taking part in as, once admitted to a 'comparsa', if they would have me, I would instantly have twenty or thirty new friends.

Under Gerald's critical scrutiny I merely said, "Hmm," but while walking Sancho I mused on this idea and came to the conclusion that while the Easter processions would be out of bounds to a Protestant, and the Moors and Christians fiesta does not really appeal to me, there must be *some* organisation which I could join. I will put my thinking cap on and also ask Paco, Andy, Trevor and Alfredo - my only friends to date - to don theirs.

On my return, Gerald was putting the finishing touches to a rack inside the goat house on which to place the hay, but neither hay nor grain could tempt Ernestina to enter, and it was only by nibbling at a carrot in front of her and throwing it inside that I could induce her to step in. She snatched up the carrot and shot out again before I had time to block her exit and I do feel that she is rather ungrateful after all the effort we have put into building her house. When it rains she will see the light, figuratively speaking.

My egg tally is now a fairly constant five or six per day - approximately 2:1 hen to turkey eggs - and when Lena and

Gerald have left we will struggle to eat them all. I pointed this out to Pamela and she thought that Esme would be willing to buy some from us. On asking her who this Esme was, she said, "The nice lady in the shop," and I racked my brains as to who this nice lady could be, before realising that it must be the old crone who eyes me so suspiciously. Pamela says that she is lovely and suggested that I accompany her to the shop when we have a dozen eggs to spare, so that she will see that I have a wife and am not a weird interloper. She added that Esme was very traditional and a firm believer in 'mal de ojo' (the evil eye) and it would be as well to assure her that I had not cast mine upon her. I said that it seemed more likely that she had cast hers upon me and, if so, she could jolly well uncast it as it may well explain the latest crop of pitifully shrivelled aubergines.

Domingo, 7 de Septiembre

Today being Gerald and Lena's last day, I decided to ask his advice on my autumn planting and also suggest some additions to his wardrobe. I deemed it wiser to address the horticultural issue first and he told me that when the last few tomatoes and peppers had been picked I should pull everything up and chuck it in the composter - such a lot of green matter! - before borrowing Andy's rotavator and ploughing it all over. He said that I could plant broad beans, turnips, carrots, spinach, radish, broccoli, cabbage, sprouts, leeks and celery, and, on seeing my startled expression, he asked, "Are you a 'liver off the land' like you keep saying, or what?" I said that I was indeed dead set on self-sufficiency, but that after last winter's poor harvests, I hadn't thought of planting so many things. He replied that I had started too late last year and that most of his suggestions will have yielded before the really cold weather sets in. Thus convinced, I jotted down all of his suggestions, before he took my pad to write my instructions for the shed foundations.

Still recovering from the shock of having to plant so many items, my rapid mental calculation of the amount of digging and concrete mixing that the foundations would entail must have caused my face to fall somewhat, as he then added, to my only partial surprise, "I might be down here to give you a hand at some point, anyway." "But," I said, adopting my best puzzled look, "you will be in Australia, won't you?" to which he replied that this was now by no means certain, as Lena had begun to express some reservations about making the trip and that he didn't want to go without her lest 'some other bloody hippy' snatch her away from him. "One day she was all for it," he said, "and the next she was going on about all the creepy-crawlies that are out there. It's very strange." I sympathised and reminded him of the fickleness of the female brain, before going straight to my study to destroy the photos. I sincerely hope that Lena has the good sense never to mention them during my lifetime.

To cheer him up I decided that we would lunch at Paco's brother-in-law's restaurant on the road to Villeda, where Gerald was welcomed with open arms by the owner, Pepe, who told him that his vegetarian suggestions had been a great success, especially with the foreigners. We all partook of the 'Revuelto Gerardo' and the 'Lasaña Pamela' that he had invented on his first visit and he glowed with pride. I thought the moment of our return home an auspicious one in which to bring down the three shirts, trousers and jacket which I told him I no longer wore and which he might find useful, someday, perhaps. He laughed and said that he doubted very much that he would ever wear such 'capitalist fancy dress', but that he would take a couple of shirts and the trousers in case Lena's father dropped dead on seeing him and he had to attend the funeral. Lena said that the beige shirt was very nice, so there may be light at the end of their nonconformist tunnel after all.

Martes, 9 de Septiembre

The happy couple left for Germany yesterday afternoon, both of them with our blessing and Gerald with his wallet full of the euros which I had given him, partly in thanks for his invaluable advice and assistance and partly to enable him to make a good impression on his future parents-in-law.

Gerald insisted on a family meditation session before their departure, so we adjourned to the living room and took our positions; the three of them cross-legged on the floor and me seated rather conspicuously on a dining chair, but keeping my back very straight and my palms upwards. After we had done the usual breathing rigmarole, my thoughts, as if by magic, transported themselves back to the last session I took part in, when the idea of creating a pond occurred to me.

While still eager to install an attractive water feature, I felt that the shed must take precedence due to its more utilitarian nature, so - ignoring Gerald's instructions to focus on a small white cloud floating across an otherwise clear blue sky - I meditated on this for a while and came to the conclusion that once the shed was in place there would be very little space for anything else. I then pondered on how best to approach Pedro and Rocío regarding my possible purchase of their plot, before turning my thoughts to the legal issues involved in such an acquisition. By the time Gerald told us that the session was over and complimented me on my much improved concentration, I had decided to first approach Miguel - my interpreter and ostensible 'enchufe' (connection) at the town hall - as to how best to go about the expansion of Integración once the deceased ex-owner's errant sister had been pinned down, figuratively speaking, and made to sign over the deeds to *my* land.

I found the session very helpful, but now that Pamela and I are alone once more, I doubt that I will find the time to meditate again until I have cleared, ploughed and replanted the plot. Our classes also recommence this week, after the short sabbatical which Pamela insisted on in order to maximise her time with her son, and I must prepare more flash cards. Life isn't easy when one strives to be a horticulturalist, livestock rearer and pedagogue all at the same time. My job in the City and, on reflection, lack of any other duties whatsoever, seems like a loafer's life to me now.

Speaking of my esteemed wife, she is also very pleased that it seems increasingly unlikely that Gerald will return to Australia and if she suspects any foul play on my part, she has made no mention of it. I do hope that Lena keeps stumm on the subject of the photos or my twilight years may not be worth living. I checked that Gerald had packed his new clothes in his rucksack and I could swear that Lena had lopped a couple of inches off his ponytail, so all augurs as well as can be expected for his introduction into the Krankl household. I am also almost sure that he is beginning to lose that awful Australian accent, which is a great relief to me.

Jueves, 11 de Septiembre

After eavesdropping on Pamela's teenage class on Tuesday night, in which a smattering of the conditional tense was to be heard, I was determined to resume my adult class with a vengeance in order to stay well ahead of the teeny-bumpkins. We commenced proceedings with a thorough revision of all of the flashcards I have introduced to date, and all except Francisco responded well. He seemed decidedly preoccupied and answered very quietly if he answered at all, in marked contrast to our last class in which the effect of me having told him, falsely of course, that he was my best student produced a suppressed euphoria most conducive to the wellbeing of the rest of us.

After forty gruelling minutes of flashcard drilling, which produced a bead of perspiration upon my friend Paco's left temple - only the second time I have seen a Spaniard sweat - I put away the cards amid sighs of relief and asked them what they had done since our last meeting. My star pupil Lola, who tricked her way into the beginners' class after decades of surreptitious studies, said that she had been embroidering a shawl, had taken a refreshing stroll most evenings, and had thoroughly enjoyed her town's Moors and Christians festival. I translated this, with some difficulty, for the rest of the class and vowed afresh to establish a more advanced class for this benign imposter, before moving on to Marta, the sociology graduate/checkout girl. Her, "I worked hard and I listened to music and I baked cakes," followed by the similarly correct but reassuringly uninspired utterances of her husband Jorge, proved to be the middle ground between Lola and Paco, whose, "I been drive tractor fields and eating foods and drunked small beer and not go Moor fiesta stupid," brought home to me the vast spectrum of linguistic talent which I had before me.

This inopportune state of affairs, however, paled into insignificance when Francisco told us, and I do not quote verbatim, that he was worried that he was going to lose his job because the new office manager did not like him. Amid general and sincere concern, he switched to Spanish - something normally punishable by my most withering glare, but now overlooked due to the gravity of the situation - and told us that this fat little Franco lookalike did not appreciate his innocent jests, such as unplugging his computer or putting salt in his coffee, which the former incumbent, knowing Francisco's history of mental unusualness, had tolerated. Francisco then told us that, rather than refraining from further pranks, something in his head had told him to continue to annoy the little man by wearing odd socks, answering the telephone in English, and using an old soup tin as a water glass. Lola remonstrated that he simply must cut out this nonsense and behave normally, to which Francisco replied that he was trying and that the official warning that he had received had shocked him into a rigid conformity which he had now kept up for two days. "But," he said, unexpectedly lapsing into English, "I think something go bad soon. My head feel want to explode. I very worry." We tried to reassure him as best we could and Paco very kindly promised to meet him at lunchtime the next day to run through some ideas that might help him to keep his job.

Later, after pouring out two small glasses of our habitual almond liqueur, I asked Paco what ideas he intended to propose to Francisco. He confessed that he had none as yet and had hoped that the two of us might come up with some, adding that, "La esperanza es lo último que se pierde." This means, I think, that hope is the last thing one should lose, and after much fruitless debate we concluded that the only hope was for Francisco's brain to make one of its periodic adjustments or for the manager to leave. Later, as we crooned along to Hank Williams' 'I'm Sorry For You My Friend', I am sure that both our thoughts were with our poor, deranged, classroom comrade.

As I reread and put the finishing touches to this lengthy and, I must say, powerfully descriptive journal entry, I hear Pamela's kiddies' class thundering down the stairs after what sounded like another lively and carefree lesson. My wife is lucky not to have to deal with the challenges of the more complex and peculiar minds of some adult students.

Sábado, 13 de Septiembre

Today I took part in my first game of golf for six weeks and, although the slightly cooler weather did much to increase my energy levels, Alfredo's extra practice made him unassailable, despite my unrelenting monologue on the English-speaking back nine. My opponent's quip on holing a four yard putt at the eighteenth of, "Even so much talking cannot distract Alfredo the Great," suggests that his linguistic game is also improving and I may suggest that he team up with Lola in a new Advanced English class, if I can find a way of fitting it into my busy schedule.

In the clubhouse today over our cold beers, I asked him to suggest possible organisations which I could join in order to meet more natives and thus improve my Spanish and integrate even more than I have done already. He warned me against the Moors and Christians 'comparsas', as they were, he said, hives of jealousy, one-upmanship and drunkenness, but he heartily recommended his Easter procession 'cofradía', saying that it was a fine body of mostly prosperous, not at all envious, and hardly ever drunken fellows that the other townsmen would murder their mothers to get into. When I reminded him that I was a non-practicing Church of England Protestant, he laughed and replied that actual church-going was not high on the group's agenda during the rest of the year and that, so long as I was some kind of Christian, he could get me voted in. He went on to say that it was also much cheaper than the Moors and Christians, but when he told me the annual subscription fee - more than my golf club membership in England - I begged him to remember that I was but a poor subsistence farmer and would prefer to join an organisation that did not involve so much dressing up, wining and dining, and - I implied rather than said - pomposity.

After much thinking and head scratching he said that he believed that in Villeda there was a cycling club, a running club, a football club, a tennis club and a hunting society; the latter having more members than all the others put together. "All sport and killing!" I said, to which he replied, "What else do men do?" I shall have to ask my students if they know of any indigenous cultural, artistic, historical, or even handicraft clubs in the town, as surely man cannot live on sport alone.

Alfredo then said that while we were on the subject of killing, which I didn't know we were, he had been given two tickets to the bullfight in Lorca, Murcia, for the following Sunday and didn't know who to give them to, as he was not especially keen on the supposed 'fiesta nacional'. I replied that while not keen on killing as a rule, being as I was a vegetarian whenever my son was at home, I felt that I simply must attend a bullfight in order to make my mind up as to just how barbaric they really were. He asked me if I had not seen one on television and I said that I had, to which he replied, "That's how barbaric they are; ni más, ni menos." (Neither more nor less.)

After much friendly banter and a call to Pamela on Alfredo's mobile telephone - a device that a rustic like myself should and will not possess - to confirm her expected refusal to attend such a 'repulsive blood-fest', I finally persuaded Alfredo to accompany me to the event which would set me even further apart from the squeamish expats who, while happy enough to munch enormous hamburgers, no doubt consider a bullfight merely an excuse to torture animals, instead of the artistic display of manliness which the aficionados in the dirty bar assure me it is. We will go in Alfredo's splendid air-conditioned car and his only stipulation is that I invite him to lunch in the best restaurant in Lorca; cheaper, surely, than the 200 mile round trip in my guzzling beast.

Ernestina has still not deigned to enter her lovingly constructed winter quarters, but tomorrow's forecast of the long awaited autumn rains will no doubt see her scurrying gratefully for cover.

Domingo, 14 de Septiembre

After much talk in the dirty bar after lunch of the torrential rains which are expected, the few drops which have fallen this afternoon make me suspect that the Spaniard does not know what a real downpour is. None of the predicted spring deluges ever materialised in this part of the country and I doubt that today's dramatic forecast will produce more than a few inconsequential showers, which is all that I desire as it will soon be time to rip up the old and prepare the land for the new.

Lunes, 15 de Septiembre

I was awoken at half past five this morning by the torrential rain beating on the bedroom window, so I got up, found my torch, and stepped out onto the patio to investigate the extent of the rainfall, before stepping back into the kitchen and kicking off my sodden sandals. My torch revealed an inch of swirling water on the patio and a plot that was entirely submerged; the water almost reaching the level of the chicken coop floor. I aimed my torch across to the goat pen and focussed on Ernestina, standing out in the open, knee deep in water and eying me malevolently.

I returned upstairs with my camera to immortalise the first calamity of my fledgling farmer's life, waking Pamela in the process and producing the morning greeting of, "Shut the sodding window, you fool." I am a farmer, but Pamela cannot yet be said to be a farmer's wife as, instead of springing out of bed and rushing to help me save my stricken livestock, she rolled over and pulled my pillow over her head. Thus unaided, I put on my wellington boots and mackintosh and waded out into the dark and stormy night to rescue my goat. Ernestina, however, instead of slipping her head into the lovingly tendered noose of rope, splashed off into her house - quite possibly for the first ever time - and would not be budged. After telling her that she was like a bloody goat and perceiving for the first time the real accuracy of this expression, I waded over to the chicken coop and shone my torch inside. All the birds seemed oblivious to their perilous situation - two more inches of water would see them awash - and only one turkey opened its eyes and gave the torch a half-hearted peck before nodding off again.

When I returned to the house to assess the situation, I realised that Sancho, who had been observing my movements with polite interest, was nowhere to be seen. Fearing him drowned, I rushed outside and shone my torch up and down the plot until I picked him out paddling past the tomatoes towards where the spinach lay submerged; swimming, it appeared, purely for pleasure. While I allowed him to get his morning exercise in this manner - just as well, for there was little likelihood of walking today - I sawed a plank on the patio before striking out once more for the chicken coop to nail it across the bottom of the door.

By the time I returned to the kitchen, my left wellington boot now full of water after foolishly kneeling to hammer in the nails, Pamela had arisen and was preparing a much needed cup of tea. As it was seven o'clock - almost two hours before her usual townsperson's getting up time - I concluded that she had finally reacted to the urgency of the situation. When I told her that Ernestina was preparing to turn her house into a mausoleum and our hens and turkeys were also in danger of extinction, she nodded and, after stirring the tea most nonchalantly for a while, said, "Well, leave the goat pen open so that she can choose life if she wishes, and pile up all those old bricks and other stuff outside the coop so that they have somewhere to stand."

Brilliant! After drinking my tea and eating two of the rogue crumpets which Pamela obtained from Nerys and smuggled into the house - foreign food, but delicious - I told my wife that I might be some time and plunged out into the tempest once more. I opened Ernestina's gate and told her she could come out if she wished, before beginning to lug bricks over to the chicken coop. With every extremity now soaked, I was counting the minutes until Nora's wrinkly face popped up over the fence, when who should appear over the other fence, but Pedro, under an umbrella and enveloped in a cloud of noxious smoke. When he giggled and disappeared from view, I could but curse that pot smoking gypsy to whom my catastrophe was merely a source of amusement and who, if it wasn't for his good fortune at being able to play the guitar so well, would be hawking socks on a market stall.

Shortly afterwards I had reason to retract these somewhat prejudiced thoughts when he called me to the fence and helped me to hoist over a large coffee table, two chairs, and the car bonnet which I had once used to construct a punishment cell for the turkeys. He told me to make a platform outside the entrance to the coop, weigh it down with bricks, and then to string some rope across the corners of the fencing for them to perch on. Brilliant! Perhaps the stuff that he smokes really does provide the inspiration for all things musical, artistic and practical that Andy claims it does, although, as I later said to Pamela, I would have come up with a similar solution eventually without the aid of illegal substances. "Yes," she replied, "just in time to lay out the corpses," which I thought rather harsh after my traumatic and exhausting morning.

To add insult to injury, the rain abated in the afternoon and at the time of writing the water level has subsided considerably, leaving my car boot and coffee table platform looking rather ridiculous as the birds patter and peck around and under it. Ernestina, after eventually leaving her flooded house and catching up on her sleep on the patio, spent the rest of the afternoon trudging round the plot and nibbling away at what remains of my crops. I don't care now, as when the plot eventually dries out - hopefully before Christmas - it is all going into the composter. The only animal feed that has survived the deluge is the hay on the rack which Gerald constructed in the goat house, so sandwich boxes have again been resorted to for their temporary sustenance. I would certainly not like to farm somewhere where it rains all the time, such as Bangladesh or Lancashire.

Jueves, 18 de Septiembre

Much to report in my journal, as for the last three days the weather has dictated most of my considerable range of activities. On the morning after the first torrential downpour, while I was cleaning out the pen and coop, I felt Nora's presence over the fence and turned to see him staring wide-eyed at my flood relief structure, looking for all the world like the gibbering senile wretch that I fear he is fast becoming. I pointed to yesterday's waterline an inch below the doorway and, as I had yet to speak, it occurred to me to play him at his own game and rely solely on mime. I pointed to the entrance to the coop and raised my hand to represent the water rising, before clutching my throat to represent suffocation, in this case by drowning. I then walked my fingers onto the coffee table and across to the car bonnet, before perching my hand on one of the ropes I had secured across the fence and moving it around in a fowl-like fashion. I gave him the thumbs up sign and he nodded noncommittally, before saying - actually *saying* - that the water always receded as quickly as it rose and that, in any case, despite the forecast of more rain for the afternoon, he was sure that I could now dispense with my little 'portaaviones' (aircraft carrier) as the worst was now over.

Stunned by this lengthy speech into a prolongation of my silence, I gave him the thumbs up once more, before beginning to cart the components of my platform out of the enclosure, during which time he kept up a constant monologue about the 'inundaciones de verdad' (real floods) that had occurred during his seventy-six years spent in his house. Finally, unable to contain myself, I said, "Ah, entonces tienes setenta y seis años?" ('Ah, so you are seventy-six?') to which he responded by shaking his finger and writing seventy-eight in the air. I despair of ever having a conversation with this man, but was pleased to hear that he is slightly older than I thought.

On Tuesday night and all day yesterday more rain fell, keeping me indoors, along with Sancho who appears to like mud even more than water and, Pamela having tired of constantly mopping the kitchen floor, is not allowed on the plot until further notice. This confinement - mine, not Sancho's - enabled me to write more flashcards in an attempt to catch up with Pamela's astounding output.

It was with some trepidation that I and my four sane students awaited the arrival of Francisco yesterday evening, and it wasn't until ten past seven that a gentle knock on the classroom door signalled his arrival. I put down my new 'Grocer's Shop' flashcards and asked him how he was. "I still in job," he replied, "by the hairs." My students sighed and tutted sympathetically and, noting my perplexity, Lola said, "He means 'just about' or 'by the skin of his teeth'." I thanked her, reminded myself to establish my new advanced group before she completely undermines my linguistic authority, and then allowed Francisco two minutes of Spanish to apprise us of the situation. It transpires that, despite having his mother check his clothing each morning for eccentricities and also being able to count on his colleagues' assistance in keeping his desk free from foreign objects, nobody but himself can control what comes out of his mouth. After a series of unfortunate ripostes in reply to the office manager's instructions, he decided that the best policy was to keep his mouth shut, and since Tuesday morning he had uttered not a single word in his presence. Nods, shakes of the head and thumbs up signs had sufficed so far, but he feared that this had only increased the nasty little man's desire to have him removed.

After words of encouragement from all of us, we returned to the sliced ham, scotch eggs and pickled gherkins of the grocer's shop and were progressing well until Lola interrupted me to ask if it was strictly necessary to learn about pints, pounds and ounces if, as she was led to believe, they had already been phased out. I told her in no uncertain terms that, while we were now forced to make our purchases in the odious kilogrammes and litres, all mature, civilised English people still *thought* in pounds, gallons, pints and even ounces and that any serious English scholar should learn them. I also decided on the spot that any student who knew the term 'phased out' ought to be immediately phased out of a beginners' group and I asked her to stay behind to speak to me after the class.

That put paid to her interruptions and she answered in a very subdued manner for the rest of the class, even making mistakes - intentional, I am sure - in a vain attempt to avoid the banishment that she feared. When the other students had left the room and before she had time to burst into tears, I asked her if she was free on Monday evenings. She said that she was and I then congratulated her on becoming the first member of the new Advanced Class which would commence the week after next. Delighted by this news, she asked me how many students there would be in the class, but my reply of, "Between one and two to begin with," somewhat diminished her joyfulness. "But it will grow," I said encouragingly, which I hope it will as I now have an extra class to prepare and deliver for no extra money. I shall beseech Alfredo to come and will also write a suitable advertisement.

On apprising Pamela of my decision to form an elite group of students, she laughed and asked me if our ten available classroom chairs would be enough. She seems to share Trevor and Janice's opinion that Villeda and its surrounding villages are a cultural and intellectual wasteland, but I intend to prove her wrong by recruiting other closet anglophiles like Lola and, hopefully, Alfredo. When I told her about the imperial measures dispute which led to my flash decision, she laughed again and asked me why I was such a staunch defender of the customs of a country in which I never intended to live again. Having no ready answer to this question and tiring of being a constant source of amusement, I retired to my study to look up 'Advanced English Classes' on the internet; research into which has occupied most of my time today. I shall write more on this fascinating subject when I have decided from which angle to approach these challenging classes.

Sábado, 20 de Septiembre

The plot having now dried out enough to dispense with my wellington boots, today I began to uproot the remains of my summer crops and gorge my composter with its long awaited green matter. Pamela protested that there were still tomatoes growing, but when I pointed out the vital necessity of carrying out my autumn planting as soon as possible, she didn't demur. I think she is as fed up of eating them every day as I am and we have many frozen ones in the freezer. Alas, too late in the summer I discovered the simple technique of sun-drying them which neither Andy, Paco, Gerald nor Nora had bothered to tell me about. In the not too distant future I shall have every reason to consider myself a self-taught horticulturalist.

The forecast is set fair for tomorrow - the day of my first ever bullfight.

Lunes, 22 de Septiembre

Yesterday I spent a pleasant day with my friend Alfredo, marred only by witnessing my last ever bullfight and a single disagreeable moment in the restaurant. Rather, however, than viewing the day in retrospect and appearing to pass judgement right away, I will take the future reader through my range of impressions and emotions as the day progressed and then pass judgement.

After a delightfully smooth drive down the mercifully - for Alfredo - toll-free motorway from Alicante, we arrived at the historic town of Lorca shortly after one o'clock, giving us time before lunch for a pleasant stroll along the old streets below the castle and a peek into a church or two. Our appetites thus whetted, we entered the restaurant of Alfredo's choice and took our seats at our reserved table in the crowded dining room. Most of the other diners were fellow bullfighting aficionados, identifiable, Alfredo explained, by their smart dress, refined table manners, and haughty demeanour. We too had dressed smartly and I instantly felt at home among these upper middle class people of whom I was once one - and still am if I choose to be.

We ate a lengthy meal comprising: typical Lorca salad (salad), 'gazpacho' (cold tomato soup ruined by the garlic and by being cold), typical Lorca fried artichokes (delicious), 'Huevas de Mújol' (like caviar and just as revolting), 'Olla Gitana' ('Gypsy Stew' - tasty despite the chickpeas) and 'Higos de Higuera' ('Figs of the Fig Tree' - where else?). We also consumed almost two bottles of fine red wine chosen by Alfredo which, combined with the preliminary glasses of beer, made me feel quite exhilarated and encouraged me to broach the subject of English classes. As we had spoken in English on the drive down and in Spanish during lunch, I cunningly switched back to English over coffee and asked him to run through the various phases of the bullfight for me once more. He got as far as, "The bull run out very fast and angry and see bullfighter with his - how you say 'capote'?" before then stumbling over every third word until he ground to a halt and bowed his head over his huge brandy glass. "Your English is getting better," I said, "but I think that after a few months of classes you would speak like a native."

Suspecting nothing mendacious in this statement - and I had not specified a native of which country - he smiled shyly, went a little redder than he had already become, and after two minutes of unassailable reasoning had promised that he would be at Integración at seven o'clock sharp a week on Monday. Brilliant! My humble rusticity has not diminished my powers of persuasion which came in so useful in my City days and propelled me into a mid-management position a full eight months short of my fortieth birthday. I proposed a toast, "To Alfredo, soon to be the greatest English speaking Spaniard in the Villeda district," and we clinked glasses and finished our brandy, before I pulled the little tray holding the bill towards me and opened it with a flourish.

Pamela says that I am hopeless at concealing my emotions, and my reaction on seeing the price was something akin to that of a deep sea diver touching the seabed and realising that he has left his oxygen bottle on the boat. Unwilling, however, to dampen our jolly post-lunch camaraderie, I inhaled deeply, exhaled very slowly through my nostrils, and took out my wallet. By comparison, the Parador restaurant at Cuenca seemed like the corner chip shop of my youth and I plonked down my bank card with a mixture of resignation and outrage (30/70). Alfredo thanked me politely, the shadow of a smile playing on his face, and said that there was nothing better than Huevas de Mújol washed down by an excellent red to put one in the mood for an afternoon of sporting butchery.

I quickly recovered my composure as we made our way

towards the bullring and, on taking our seats in the shaded part of the noble amphitheatre - the best seats rather than the worst as my still partially English mind had assumed - the thrill of the occasion erased all memory of the scandalous bill from my mind. The brass band struck up and all the bullfighters entered the ring, looking very dignified despite their effeminate clothing, and walked across to salute the 'Presidente', before most of them slipped behind the wooden barriers to await their prey from positions of safety. When the huge bull thundered out into the ring, one could but admire the courage of a man prepared to try to stick a sword between the horns of such a colossus, but in my previous television viewing I had clearly not paid much attention, for while the bull was in this rampant state there were in fact three bullfighters who took turns at calling the beast towards their large pink and yellow capes, making jolly sure that there was plenty of cape between themselves and the bull's horns.

It was, nevertheless, an extremely sporting spectacle - most amusing when one of the men had to vault over the barriers to safety - and I was looking forward to the principal torero, identifiable by his especially twinkly jacket, getting down to business and risking his life for our entertainment. When the two stout horsemen appeared, the bull now had something more solid to aim at and charged heartily into the heavily protected side of one of them, only for the rider to plunge his lance into its back and spend a good while pushing and twisting it about. This took place only twenty yards from our seats and the gush of blood that was produced sobered me somewhat and made me feel that this was not quite playing the game; even less so when the other horseman, after inviting the dumb beast to charge him, leant even more heavily and spent even longer digging his spear into the bull.

Alfredo, by contrast, was warming to the occasion and, noting my concern, told me not to worry as the horses didn't feel a thing, unlike in the olden days when they had no protection and their guts spilled out onto the sand. Suppressing the rising taste of garlic in my throat, I agreed that this new-fangled padding was very considerate, but that it was the bull who seemed to be getting rather a raw deal. "Yes," he replied, "he calm down a bit now."

When the mounted butchers had left the ring, the bull was left to ponder awhile, until one of the less gaudy bullfighters picked up a pair of colourful sticks called 'banderillas' and wandered out into the centre, before lifting the sticks and running round in little circles to attract the beast's attention. It roused itself from its thoughts - of sunny meadows and its harem of cows, no doubt - to charge the prancing man, who drew it away before turning to plunge the barbed poles into its upper back, producing fresh rivulets of blood. I considered that to be quite enough handicapping for one day and thought it was about time for the main bullfighter to show his mettle while the bull still had enough blood to keep its legs going, but, alas, five more pairs of skewers were thrust into the poor creature before he was left alone again.

At this point a bugle sounded to signal that the third part of the fight was to begin and the bullfighter walked out proudly with his sword and smaller red cape to much applause. By now the bull, his head very low and blood streaming down his haunches, appeared less than keen to receive further punishment, but they are not called 'toros bravos' for nothing and, after much cape waving, the bullfighter persuaded him that he might still be able to dig his horns into one of his tormentors, so he charged anew. Alfredo said that this was where the real spectacle began and it is true that the man got quite close to the bull's horns, coaxing him around his body with his cape very skilfully, before stepping aside to the applause of the crowd while the bull got what was left of his breathe back. From my point of view, however, this was no longer cricket, figuratively speaking, if it ever had been, and I would have much rather he had got down to business in this manner right from the start. I shared my thoughts with Alfredo, who laughed and said that, while it would make excellent entertainment, the country's bullfighting schools would struggle to keep up with demand for new toreros every weekend and that the profession would lose its appeal very quickly. So be it, I thought.

When the bullfighter had ensured that the bull was practically comatose, he took his stance, raised his sword, and plunged it right into the bull's neck, causing the beast to give a jolt and die, it appeared, on its feet. The applause was tremendous and Alfredo said above the racket that it had been an excellent kill and that the torero would get at least one ear, if not two, in recognition of his skilful work with the cape and his swift despatch of the noble beast which had ended its suffering so humanely. I clapped politely, mainly due to my desire not to draw attention to myself, but felt quite sad when the bull was later dragged out of the ring by a team of horses, leaving a trail of blood in his wake. Seeing the bullfighter holding the ears aloft and receiving the applause of these otherwise smart, civilised people put the final nail in the bullfighting coffin, so to speak, for me.

I felt quite drained and ready to leave until Alfredo reminded me that there were *five* more bulls to be killed - two for each of the three main toreros - and I slumped back into my seat. Noting my poorly hidden lack of enthusiasm, he said that just seeing each of the toreros perform once would satisfy his bloodlust for one year, so I had only two more slaughters to witness, the last of which ended grotesquely due to the torero repeatedly failing to hit the mark and eventually having to resort to a dagger with which to execute the moribund creature, much to the disapproval of the crowd. At least the dead bull kept its ears, which made me wonder what the first torero would do with his. Stuff them? I don't know and hardly care.

On leaving the arena Alfredo suggested a refreshing drink before we took to the road, so we entered a bar where he promptly ordered a whisky and coke. I expressed concern that he was about to drive 150 kilometres, but Alfredo explained that on such a straight motorway his car practically drove itself and the coke would stop him feeling sleepy. I ordered a 'café solo' and a glass of water for myself in order to remain vigilant and asked him if he had really enjoyed the bullfight. He said that watching a 'corrida de toros' produced in him a curious mixture of exhilaration and 'verguenza' (shame) which never occurred in normal life and that he thought was, perhaps, a kind of throwback to more primitive times, before man had become the supreme predator and when life was a constant battle for survival. I thought this most eloquent and on the drive back I mused upon it until I dozed off. On awaking as we neared the village, I reflected that what he had said was balderdash and I told him so. He replied,

"Balderdash, what is?"

"Tonterías"

"I know. It just excuse. Perhaps I don't go to toros no more."

Jueves, 25 de Septiembre

As Monday's epic descriptive and philosophical journal entry used up the rest of my ink, today I resume the routine reportage of the practical farmer and teacher wielding a basic ballpoint pen. Having finally cleared the plot of its summer growth, my composter is now so full to the brim with green matter that there is no room for any more brown matter. I will ask Andy if it matters so much if the matters are not evenly matched when he brings the rotavator round next week. (Revise: too many matters.)

Yesterday's class passed off without any major upsets as Francisco is still clinging to his job with the help of his mother and his loyal colleagues and says that he has recovered the power of speech in the presence of the office manager, albeit only to say, 'sí', 'no', and 'no he sido yo' (it wasn't me). As it was to be Lola's last lesson with her less gifted classmates, she asked permission to recite a little poem at the end of the class by way of thanking us all - the teacher especially, I think - for the wonderful classes that she had enjoyed. I reproduce it here to illustrate what my students are capable of after only five months under my tutelage.

A happy day it was when I,
Entered Integration,
Ernesto held his cards up high,
We answered as one nation.

He taught us all to pronounce well,

And shouted if we didn't,
Which may sound like a students' hell,
But we did as we were bidden.

Us just folk of a Spanish town,
We spoke up clear and sweet,
Afraid of earning a nasty frown,
Or a stamp of Ernesto's feet.

So thank you Ernesto, Paco and Marta,
Francisco and Jorge too,
My time with you I would not alter,
But now I must go through,

To the advanced class with brilliant students,
Where Lola will try so hard,
To say so well, so wise, so prudent,
The answer to each flashcard.

We all applauded this sterling effort and I laughed at her playful suggestion that I was a rather strict teacher, before beginning to translate it for the others. Lola confessed that she had made full use of her thesaurus and that it had taken her seven hours to compose, so after I had stumbled through the first stanza I allowed her to render it quickly into Spanish rather than eat into precious almond liqueur time. The rest of the class dismissed, Paco and I settled down to a little Willie Nelson while I read through Lola's poem which she had been kind enough to print out for us all, chuckling over the 'brilliant students' who she expects to meet in the Advanced Class. She is also very much mistaken if she thinks I am going to create advanced flashcards for just the two of them. We will merely converse in class and I will set them some of the horrendously difficult exercises and reading comprehensions which I have found on the internet. Even if I were to charge Alfredo - which I shall not do due to the fact that playing golf at his club doesn't cost me a penny - it would take me months to claw back the cost of that lunch in Lorca which I have now put out of my mind, but which keeps popping back into it from time to time. Was taking me there and having me pay some kind of test? I know that Spanish men take pride in splashing out lavishly, so perhaps he thought I would enjoy flexing my spending muscles in this way. If he did, he was mistaken, but I will not bore the future reader with this trifling subject any more, as it is now merely euros under the bridge for me.

Domingo, 28 de Septiembre

On Friday we received the first news from Gerald since his departure for Germany over two weeks ago. It was an email, of course, as Gerald is not fond of telephones, and its brevity can be guessed at by the fact that Pamela tossed a printed copy of it to me screwed up in a ball. It read:

Guten abend Mutter und Vater.
Germans mostly enlightened and not so primitive as Spanish, though not as jolly. Mrs Krankl is a darling. Almost got Herr Krankl in pocket now. Language learnable. Australia off for now. Lena says hallo.
Alles liebe, Gerald

I pointed out that it contained most of the information that we required and that, all in all, it was most satisfactory; especially the reference to the fact that the trip to the bottom of the world appeared to have been postponed indefinitely. Pamela said, "Yes, as a bloody telegram it's a great effort. You can write back and ask him what he's actually *doing*," so I scuttled off to the computer to avoid any more maternal wrath and foul language; always a danger sign in my wife.

Embracing his journalistic style, I wrote:

Gutten Morgen son,
Glad all gut. Stop. Your Mutter requires minimum 500 words on your progress. Stop. Not repeat not telegram. Stop. Any ideas about work? Stop. Liebe to Lena and self from both. Full stop.

I thought this rather droll, but lingered at the machine a while longer, lest she suspect me of making a less than rigorous reply, and looked up 'flat pack sheds' on the internet. I found dozens of attractive wooden options available in England, but very few in Spain and those mostly ugly metal affairs. Postage from England would be rather expensive, however, so I shall research the matter further. I also found an interesting 'Proficiency English' reading comprehension with an extract from Huckleberry Finn and printed out three copies, but only one with the answers. I will subject Lola and Alfredo to this on Monday if our conversation dries up.

I then remembered that I had intended to write an advertisement for the Advanced Class in order to attract more students and immediately set to work. Reasoning that I only wish to attract scholars of considerable knowledge, I chose my words accordingly and this was the result of my labours:

Advanced English Classes at Integración,
Puebla de Don Arsenio
Villeda
Alicante
Spain

Due to a wholly unexpected demand for English tutelage of the highest calibre in the Villeda area, Mr Ernesto Postlethwaite has the greatest pleasure in addressing all aspirants to English excellence and inviting said linguists to present themselves at the above address on the Monday evening of their choice at 6.50pm in order to appraise the suitability of the curriculum with regard to their philological requirements.

No elementary students, foreigners, or other timewasters please.

Mr Ernesto Postlethwaite, Professor of English

This should ensure that only those with a sound basic knowledge of English will come along. 'Profesor', for the uninitiated, means teacher in Spanish, so I have indulged in a little poetic licence by referring to myself as a professor, which is so much easier to understand. It is at times like these that I regret having preferred to plunge into the competitive world of commerce rather than going to university, which I could easily have done. Now I would have a B.A. or a B.Sc. after my name, or even a Dr before it, instead of being plain Mr Postlethwaite. No matter; when these journals are finally published an honorary degree or two may well come my way.

Before describing my inaugural Advanced Class, I will first write about something more stimulating; namely this morning's second attempt to let Sancho off the lead. I reasoned that if I am to take Ernestina out to pasture in order that she may nibble some fresh food and stretch her legs, I would prefer to take Sancho too, but suspect that I will need the strength of both my arms to handle the growing goat. With this in mind, I headed for the least frequented track with a store of treats in my pocket and, after a stern lecture regarding obedience, let him loose.

With no open driveways to distract him, he gambolled around me happily enough and, on spotting a stick on the track, I waved it under his nose before throwing it among some olive trees. To my delight, he retrieved the stick and dropped it at my feet, so I threw it again. The instinct of the Working Cocker is a remarkable thing and no matter how many times I threw the stick, he always set off after it at top speed and brought it back. It being thirty years since I last played cricket - I was a competent, if somewhat over-defensive, batsman - my arm soon began to ache, so I instructed Sancho to rest easy for a while, which he was reluctant to do. Tiring eventually of having the stick clattered about my legs every dozen paces, I took it from him and placed it on the higher branches of the nearest olive tree. Now able to concentrate on something other than the stick, I walked on and thought about my autumn planting strategy for a while, until I perceived an absence of pattering feet and turned around. Sancho was now a black dot in the distance and no matter how loudly I called him he remained rooted to the spot. On retracing my steps, the spot, as I had guessed, was the olive tree and the silly mutt sat as if transfixed by the stick in its branches.

Being enthusiastic about an activity is a fine thing, but becoming obsessed by it - as Pamela often says - is not, so I was determined to nip this 'stickophilia' in the bud there and then. As the stick in the tree appeared to be 'the one', I took it and broke it into small pieces, placing each one on the track under Sancho's nose. I left him to survey the remains of his treasure and set off homeward, only for him to scamper up with the largest of the fourteen fragments between his teeth and continue to harass me with it.

They say that the best way to steer a young man away from the evils of drink is to make him so ill with it that he never wants to touch another drop, so with this in mind I scoured the nearest olive grove until I found an old branch about four feet long and weighing at least ten pounds. I carried it a few yards to draw attention to its allure, before flinging it to one side and walking on. After rounding a bend and reaching the road there was no Sancho in sight, so I sat down on a stone to await the effects of my therapy.

Alas, several minutes later, instead of welcoming a Sancho freed from the shackles of his fixation, he appeared around the bend with the branch in tow, his tail wagging furiously, inching his way towards me like a beast possessed. Exasperated by this absurd behaviour, I took up the branch and, seeing no alternative, carried it home, despite the solicitous stares of several neighbours who perhaps thought I had no money to buy firewood.

On the plus side, I now know that I can dispense with

Sancho's lead if I carry a stick, although the stress of pandering to his fetish may well outweigh any advantage gained. Also, those neighbours who saw me will hopefully spread the word that the inhabitants of Integración are not wealthy foreigners after all, but humble farmer-gatherers. The downside is that until I had broken up the branch, put it in the stove, and actually *burnt* it, Sancho would not relinquish his prize. I now live in fear of picking up anything larger than a pen within sight of him.

While the stick episode was interesting but infuriating, my first Advanced Class, after beginning promisingly enough, soon turned into a tiresome exchange of badly pronounced and grammatically flawed platitudes - my own statements apart - which made the hour seem like an age. I had imagined that we would bounce from one topic to another, only pausing for my brief corrections, but after the initial introductions any attempt to talk in more depth about any subject led either to interminable pauses or the wanton destruction of my beloved language.

While it is true that Lola is a mine of vocabulary and has an acceptable understanding of English grammar, she was unable to deliver more than one sentence at a time at speaking pace, before delving into the depths of her brain to prepare her next statement. Alfredo was not slow to fill these gaps, but his tangled web of shocking syntax and barely existent grammar made me realise that on our golfing outings I had paid little attention to these shortcomings, being more interested in the game than his chatter. To enable the future reader to imagine the suffering I endured, I have reproduced a fragment of our conversation as I remember it:

Ernesto: "Lola, what do you think of the Moors and Christians fiestas?"

Lola: (pause) "They are enjoyable and interesting to watch. (pause) I like the costumes and the music. (long pause) They enable people of town to get together and forget their (pause) quotidian worries. Is it correct to say quotidian, Ernesto, like 'cotidiano' in Spanish?"

Ernesto: "Yes, of course. Do go on." (It is, I later found.)

Lola: "When I was a little girl…" (interminable pause)

Alfredo: "Moor and Christians… What that word you tell me in golf club, Ernesto? Yes, bollocks. It bollocks and just show off and money, like say I got more than you and I better with big stupid helmet and all disgusting drunk. Semana Santa procession much better more religious, not so drinking and show off."

Lola: "But Alfredo, (pause) the two fiestas are similar in many ways. (pause) They are both expensive to take part (pause) in and many men (pause) participate in (pause) both. (pause) Is it not true?"

Alfredo: "Some men yes, but in my cofradía some do Moor and Christians only to laugh at stupids. Easter party serious business with church and pray and not fall over."

Ernesto: "Yes, thank you both. Now let's talk about cooking, shall we?"

Lola: I (pause)

Alfredo: "Wife cook. Is English lady but cook good."

After reading this fragment, the future reader will no doubt agree that for a man of my perfectionistic temperament this was indeed an agonising hour and I fear that my two 'advanced' students may not be as compatible as I thought. With just Lola I could ask her to spend the week preparing an hour long speech, set her grammar exercises, or just ask her questions and knit a jumper while I waited for the answers - if I knitted, which of course I don't. Alfredo, on the other hand, requires an intensive mental battering with flashcards before I will ever get anything coherent out of him. I set them the Huckleberry Finn reading comprehension for homework and will refrain from posting my advertisement until I have spent some time with my English teacher's thinking cap on.

Miércoles, 1 de OCTUBRE 2008

Today my last ever new month in Spain begins and I wonder why it is called Octubre (October) if 'Oct' normally signifies something to do with eight, as in octagon, rather than ten, as in the tenth month of the year. This is how a linguist's brain works, but this linguist is at his wits end vis-à-vis his two lamentable English groups which, after Monday's disastrous 'advanced class' and tonight's fiasco, are becoming a major cause for concern.

This evening was more counselling session than class as Francisco, arriving stylishly late as usual, interrupted my conjunction flashcards to tell us, "Fool man give me last aviso at work. He say one more stupid thing or speaking and I out door." After rendering this into correct English, I noticed a fearless glint in his eye suggesting that he was resigned to losing his job, but was unlikely to go quietly. There is also a full moon approaching, so I fear that next week we will have an unemployed Francisco on our hands.

Cutting short the cacophony of advice and guidance reminiscent of the pre-reformation Marcus which flooded forth from the other students, I insisted that if we were to spend the class saving Francisco's job, we would do so in English. After a moment's silence, I suggested that we each write down one really good piece of advice, after which we would resume our flashcard work. I plonked two dictionaries down on the table and went to seek out Pamela to ask her advice on my piece of advice. I found her in the kitchen and, familiar as she now is with Francisco's predicament, she said that his only hope was to get rid of the office manager before he got rid of him.

Thanking her for her logical though impractical input, I returned to the classroom to find that my students had come to the same conclusion. Marta suggested that he ask his colleagues to petition the regional manager for the newcomer's removal, while Jorge's offering was, "I agree with my woman," meaning wife, I think. Paco's stupid suggestion was that he accuse the office manager of sexual harassment, or 'gay nuisancing' as he put it, which I said that, although it might well trigger off months of inquiries in Britain, would be laughed off in this more macho, down to earth country.

Francisco thanked us for our advice and said that he would consider these options very carefully before deciding how to proceed, which sounded rather ominous to me. By half past seven I was once again able to divert my budding agony aunts to the task in hand, but despite injecting my conjunction cards with all the enthusiasm I could muster, their hearts were clearly not in it, so at five to eight I allowed them a short farewell babble, before wishing Francisco luck and shooing all but Paco out of the door.

Over our almond liqueur I begged Paco to not so much as mention Francisco or anything else remotely pertaining to the class as I was heartily 'harto' (fed up) of both subjects. Instead, I pointed out that it was Pamela's birthday on the 25th of the month, closely followed by our thirtieth wedding anniversary on the 27th and that I hoped I could count on him and Laura to help me with the preparations. Relieved to hear that Laura's aunt in Almansa was not expected to be ill on those dates and that I could rely on their full support, I relaxed with my drink while Paco chuntered through a few Johnny Cash favourites. I reflected that it would be extremely difficult to arrange a surprise party at Integración and also doubted that my catering capabilities would be adequate for an undertaking of such magnitude, so I shall be addressing Andy on the subject when he brings his rotavator round tomorrow.

Viernes, 3 de Octubre

Yesterday Andy and I took turns at rotavating the plot with his arm-wrenching 'mula mecánica' and today the land began to receive its autumn seed, over a month earlier than last year's largely unsuccessful planting. I hope that an extra month of benign sunshine will make all the difference and that the turnips, carrots, broad beans, cabbage and spinach that are already in the ground and the broccoli, sprouts and leeks that may or may not follow, will fare better than last winter's stunted spuds and midget onions. Garlic I did not plant as we already have enough bulbs in the pantry to feed a platoon of French legionaries.

Andy was most receptive to my request for assistance regarding Pamela's birthday bash and was even kind enough to suggest hosting the affair at his finca. He will, he says, rope in the culinary elements of Ana's family and all I shall have to do is tell him the approximate number of attendees and 'cough up the cash'. This is a great weight off my already over-occupied mind, proving yet again that Andy is a true friend and increasing my desire to explore Scotland and other places north of Milton Keynes when I am finally forced to visit the Old Country. A little road trip would be infinitely preferable to spending the whole time with Pamela's tiresome relatives and it makes me more determined than ever to make our next Spanish road trip even more of a success than our not entirely unsuccessful expedition into the wilds of Cuenca.

On showing Andy my green matter packed composter he said that it might get a bit smelly, but would decompose quickly and do the job just as well. No matter; the more bracing aromas on my burgeoning farm, the better!

Sábado, 5 de Octubre

On taking my seat in Alfredo's car this morning, I hoped that Monday's class would not form a major topic of our conversation as I did not wish to mix the increasingly onerous business of teaching English with the pleasure of playing golf. I needn't have worried, however, as his only reference to the class was to remark that he wasn't sure if Lola's English was advanced enough and that he feared that she might hold him back. His statement, "She talk slow and always stop. I can to talk all class, no problem," astonished, amused and distressed me in equal measure and thenceforth the subject was dropped.

I spoke little during the nine Spanish-speaking holes, preferring to concentrate on my still rusty game, and I reached the halfway point only four shots behind. Alfredo teed off from the tenth with a solid drive and then proceeded to drive me half mad with the execrable English which I had hardly noticed before I became his teacher. Every incorrect or non-existent verb, each crazy conjunction, and every missing preposition jarred my language-loving soul and, after my bunker-hopping hole in nine at the fourteenth impelled Alfredo to say, "You like Arab today; always look for sand," I deemed it expedient to don my teacher's cap, figuratively speaking, and begin to nip this linguistic diarrhoea in the bud.

Thereafter I corrected every single erroneous phrase that Alfredo uttered, which, in one way or another, was all of them, and refused to proceed with the game until he had repeated each statement correctly. In this manner I was able to claw back six shots by the end of the round, leaving me respectably close to his final score, and had finally made him realise that his English was about as advanced as that of an aged chimpanzee after a life of solitary confinement. An added bonus was that over our beer in the clubhouse he was more than happy to converse in Spanish and it was of economic matters that we spoke.

Having been so immersed in my autumn planting, I have had little time to pay attention to the outside world, so it was with some consternation that I received the news of the recent collapse of important American banks, the plummeting Dow Jones index, and the subsequent 700 billion dollar bailout, all of which, Alfredo assured me, will deliver the long expected 'coup de grâce' to the teetering Spanish economy and send the country back into the poverty to which it had so long been accustomed. Why my thoughts immediately turned to house prices and, more specifically, the potential fall in the price of *my* house, I do not know, as Integración is worth more than mere money to me now, so I unselfishly turned my thoughts to the fate of others and asked Alfredo if an economic crash would affect him very badly.

"Oh no," he said, switching unexpectedly to 'sotto voce' English, "lot of bankrupts mean lot of work for lawyers who know lot about insolvencia," and with a sweep of his hand he inferred that several of our fellow golfers might well soon be beating a path to his office door. At least this cheered him up somewhat after my laying waste to his delusions of English excellence and on the drive home he said, "Ernesto, I think I take English more serious from now. Maybe there be lot of foreign bankrupts too," which made me realise that lawyer's blood did indeed course through his veins.

Martes, 7 de Octubre

Reporting my conversation with Alfredo in Sunday night's journal entry reminded me that the deceased ex-house and plot owner's sister should now have returned from the Argentine, so I telephoned my soon to be ex-interpreter Miguel this morning to ask him if he knew of her whereabouts. Once the deeds to my beloved plot have been signed over to their true legal and spiritual owner - namely me - I shall dispense with his services in any future dealings with the ayuntamiento (town hall) as I think that Alfredo can provide all the 'enchufe' I require and will not charge me €50 for every twenty minutes of his 'friendship'. I also consider that I am now well able to fight my linguistic corner unaided and I also have Andy to fall back on should they ever try to entangle me in a web of jargonese. It is preferable, I think, to have a few influential friends than a multitude of useless one. Reassuring digression over.

Miguel, after asking after my health, Pamela's health, Sancho's health, and the wellbeing of Uncle Harold, who he helped to cure of his male menopausal exercise addiction, told me that the sister had indeed returned home, but was still in a state of mourning that appeared to preclude answering the telephone. I protested that over five months had now elapsed since the old duffer's demise and that I was jolly well fed up of waiting for the signature, cross, or fingerprint of this wretched woman who wasn't even the man's widow. Stunned, I believe, by my unusual firmness, the best reply he could muster was that he would call round to see her. "No," I insisted, "*I* will call round to see her." "She is a very tricky woman, Ernesto," he answered, to which I replied rather enigmatically, "And I can be a very tricky man, Miguel, if needs must," before wishing him a curt buenos días and hanging up.

From now on I shall fight my own land ownership battles and only call on the - unpaid - assistance of my real friends in cases of dire bamboozlement. No black-clad battle-axe shall stand between me and the integrity of Integración, oh no.

My first impulse was to drive over to Villeda immediately and thrust a pen into the old witch's hand, until I remembered that Pamela had already driven in to her Line Dancing session, so I took Sancho for a walk instead. Hoping that his limited canine memory had forgotten his stick obsession, I let him off the lead on entering the Harrisons' track and thrust my hands firmly into my trouser pockets. Alas, within a minute he returned, stick in mouth, and began to zigzag around in front of me, only pausing to look imploringly up and say, "Take it, take it. Take it and throw it!" - wordlessly, of course - until we reached the Harrisons' house and I decided to pay them a social call.

After halloing from the safety of the track over the fierce barking of the far from harmless sounding Alsatian, Trevor eventually appeared on the patio and beckoned me with a crutch. The proximity of the far from harmless looking teeth of his dog, however, meant that he had to propel his considerable bulk down the driveway to open the gate, explaining as he did so that last week's line dancing had knackered his knee and he had reluctantly given it a miss today. "It was making me feel like a young man again," he said, "until I overshot a full turn before a right step and hit the deck." I couldn't help but think that all that excess weight would indeed be difficult to halt on once being set spinning, but I just clucked sympathetically and followed him into the house. Once seated, he looked far more dignified surrounded by all his books than he must have done thundering around with all those expat women and I considered suggesting that digging up all his useless flowers and creating a productive plot like my own would be far better exercise and a far more suitable pastime for a cultured, middle-aged man.

Instead, after inviting him and Janice to Pamela's birthday party, I considerately prepared our tea and asked him his opinion on what kind of organisation I might join, apart from Line Dancing, of course, as the whole point was to mingle with local people and not to improve my knowledge of the myriad accents of the British Isles. After running through all the sporting societies which Alfredo had suggested and the dressing up activities which I had already rejected, he stirred his tea and ruminated for a while, before his eyes brightened and he said, "Claro! La Escuela de Adultos - night school. You could go to the night school at Villeda and do some sort of course."

Brilliant! On asking him what kind of courses they might do, he said he thought that things like computer studies, handicrafts and languages were more than likely to be on the curriculum and that, although classes usually commenced at the beginning of October, he was sure that they would squeeze me in. "But," he said, "I imagine that the students will be mostly women, as the local men are far too sport and fiesta obsessed to think of bettering themselves."

Not being in the least averse to most women and not yet counting any of the female species among my platonic friends, my first impulse was to leave my tea untasted and hurry home to consult the internet, but, as I thought this may be considered rather rude, I decided to make polite conversation at least until I had drunk it. Luckily I had recently leafed through Trevor's chapters of the History of Bolton and I told him that I had thought them most interesting and well-informed, which I am sure they are to any bright Boltonians, and asked him if he was writing anything at the moment. He told me that he was researching the history of Line Dancing, prior to writing a short book about how this form of country dance had spread across the world as far afield as China, Indonesia and South Korea. "Yes," he enthused, "and there's a rumour it may even be going on in *North* Korea too - on the sly, of course." He said that it was a fascinating subject and that as he felt he would struggle to become a maestro of the dancing itself, the thing for him to do was write about it. "Do what you know best, Ernest," he said as I was taking my cup into the kitchen. "That's what I always say."

After thanking him for the tea, I called Sancho and hastened home to see if I could find out what classes might be available at Villeda's Escuela para Adultos, reflecting that Trevor's sudden craze for Line Dancing was somewhat impetuous in a man of his age. On my arrival at Integración I asked Pamela, who had just returned, if she knew anything about night school classes in the town and, if so, what courses there might be. "Nerys goes to pottery class," she said, "and I know they do English, but I don't know what else." So pottery was out and so was English, unless they wished me to teach it, so I switched on the computer and typed in 'clases adulto Villeda', and what did I find? Nothing, save that the night school classes take place at the secondary school. This is typical of the underdeveloped nature of the Spanish internet and, although I yearn for a more primitive lifestyle in most respects, it is most annoying when you need to find crucial information fast.

After lunch I drove into Villeda on the pretext of visiting my beloved ferretería and, after ruling out yoga, pilates, 'cerámica' and 'punto de cruz' (cross stitching), signed up for 'informática' (computer) classes which begin a week on Thursday. On returning to the village, I saw Paco's tractor outside the dirty bar and popped in for a celebratory beer. I told him about the course and asked him if he would care to join me in brushing up his computer skills. He shook his head and, pointing to it, said that his computer was in there and that, besides, the classes would be full of women. Although I thought this rather typical of the rustic Spanish male's mentality, I was secretly glad that I was to go alone and thus increase my chances of making some new, studious, Spanish friends.

Pamela received my news with something approaching her usual scepticism and said, "I knew you had a new bee in your bonnet and wouldn't stop until you'd signed up to something. Still, a computer course could be interesting. What level is it?" Having forgotten to ascertain this minor detail, I said that it was intermediate and sincerely hope that it is. No matter; if it is not, I shall simply switch groups and Pamela will be none the wiser.

What else to report? Ah yes, I made yesterday's 'advanced class' an hour-long blur of flashcards which, while being mere revision for Lola, left Alfredo in a state of complete mental exhaustion and at least partial despondency. Only after administering a medicinal glass of almond liqueur and reminding him of the expediency of improving his English in order to ply his trade with the impending bevy of foreign bankrupts did he agree to return next week. Not until he knows all the beginners' flashcards off by heart shall his right to free speech be restored in the sanctity of the classroom. He will suffer, Lola may or may not get bored, but grammar will prevail.

Jueves, 9 de Octubre, 'El Nou d'Octubre' - Valencian Holiday

Today those of the villagers who work appeared to be on holiday, judging by the amount of drinking, smoking and bellowing going on in the dirty bar when I went there to take my after-lunch coffee. I questioned the track-tramping man, who for once had not caught me in an awkwardly expat situation, and he told me that it was 'El Día de la Communidad Valenciana', pointing to a small, ragged, red and yellow striped flag over the bar. On asking him what festivities took place on this holiday that nobody had seen fit to tell me about, he held up his brandy glass, shrugged, and said, "No trabajamos." (We don't work.) Resisting the impulse to ask him how much work he fitted in around his constant perambulations, I instead asked him if people really spoke Valenciano, and he replied that most of the villagers spoke it most of the time.

"Pero cuándo?" (But when?), I asked him, to which he responded by cupping his ear and pointing a big fat thumb over his shoulder. On listening carefully, the seemingly

Spanish speech which I heard did indeed appear to contain some strangely grunted words that were not altogether unfamiliar to me, but that had never actually been spoken *to* me in my almost year-long residence in La Puebla. On asking the reason for this, he said that it was considered more courteous to address 'forasteros' (outsiders, strangers) in Castilian Spanish and that, as the village was almost on the frontier of the Valencia region, even older people like himself spoke it reasonably well, although he thought, of course, in Valenciano. Rather nettled, I protested that I was no longer a forastero and he agreed that this was the case, but that being an extranjero (foreigner) by birth, people would assume that I preferred to be addressed in Spanish.

As luck would have it, we were joined at that moment by Paco, so, after admonishing him for not having told me about today's holiday during or after yesterday's class, I instructed him and the track-wanderer - Federico by name - to speak in Valenciano, as I was now a villager just like them and wished to be treated as such. After a long silence, Paco mumbled, "Com va, Federico?" to which Federico replied, "Bé, Paco, y tú?" "Bé," responded Paco, before they lapsed into silence once more. "Continúa, continúa!" I protested, to which Paco replied that they found it very difficult to speak in Valenciano in the presence of a non-speaker. Federico, who must be in his mid-sixties, pointed out that in Franco's day all regional languages were banned, so you had to be careful when you spoke Valenciano outside the home. Paco agreed that this habit must have stuck and that, besides, in this area they mixed in a lot of Spanish words and most people, himself included, couldn't even write it properly. Federico said that he wrote Valenciano just as well as he wrote Castellano and both he and

Paco laughed long and loud over this witticism until, on seeing that I had missed the joke, he explained that he couldn't write either language, having hardly had any schooling at all. This news, while rather saddening, was at the same time gratifying as it proves that I am indeed living in a truly rustic community on the very edge of modern civilisation.

To Paco's poorly concealed dismay, he has now been instructed to address me in Valenciano at all times until I have picked it up, which I doubt will take very long as most of the words appear to be the same as in Spanish or merely slightly shorter and gruffer versions. It will, I think, be something akin to learning Northern English.

Thus concluded today's news, I must now report on yesterday's main events, or event; namely yet another adult class in which didactic advancement was once again largely overlooked in favour of Francisco's ongoing employment saga. We managed seven minutes of clothing and footwear flashcards before his arrival was used by Jorge as an excuse to abandon his attempts to pronounce the word galoshes and ask him, "How work, Francisco?" The human enigma's reply of, "No, I don't love you," and subsequent collapse onto his chair in paroxysms of laughter put paid to our intense concentration and prompted me to give Francisco his habitual two minute of Spanish time in which to explain himself.

He had, it transpired, given some thought to Paco's 'gay nuisancing' suggestion, but had initially dismissed this tactic as being too unethical even for his unorthodox mind. Sensing, however, from the office manager's gloating glances on Monday afternoon that the dismissal process had been instigated, he found the words, "No, no te quiero," escaping loudly from his mouth in the direction of that person. During the complete and prolonged silence which this statement produced in the large office, Francisco told us that he sat staring down at his hands, before responding to the man's blurted demand for an explanation by shaking his head and saying, "No, Zeferino, no es posible," and, through his tremendous efforts to suppress a rising impulse to laugh, producing what he imagined must have been a terrible grimace on his face.

The use of his tormentor's rather unusual and until then undisclosed first name had, he felt, been a masterstroke and caused the 'cretino' to lose his nerve and stomp off into his own office; the slam of the door putting, Francisco thought, the stamp of guilt on the man as surely if he had brought him flowers or kissed him on the lips. To his office colleagues' barrage of questions he thought it best to continue the head-shaking strategy and carry on with his work. Since then the office had been a hive of speculation and at this very moment a meeting was taking place to which the manager had called all of the office staff except himself.

"I think he go or I go. The two can not stay," Francisco concluded with a shake of his head, leading me to believe that he is now so entrenched in the role of recipient of unrequited love that his loopy mind now believes it to be true. After this bizarre disclosure and the ensuing questions and comments which I bullied them to at least attempt to say in English, they found it extremely difficult to settle down once again to our footwear cards and I sincerely hope that by next week this soap opera will have reached its conclusion, one way or another.

While I was pouring out our almond liqueur, Paco returned to the topic of Francisco's outrageous, though truly inspired, manoeuvre with glee until I reminded him that I wished him to address me in his mother - and father - tongue from now on. He duly complied, but after continuing sheepishly for a short time he exclaimed, "Che, Ernesto, açò es molt difícil!" ('I say, Ernest, this is very difficult!') before switching back into Spanish to plead that I settle for a few phrases from time to time, rather than subjecting him to the torture of speaking Valenciano to a Castellano speaker. Seeing his sincere distress and somewhat mollified by him deeming me practically a native Spanish speaker, I agreed to his request, but asked him to say just one more thing in Valenciano before I put on the Bobbie Gentry CD which he had brought from his interminable collection of country music. He obliged me by saying, "Val, Ernesto. Fa temps que no traduïm una cançó de country i western," ('Ok, Ernest. It has been a long time since we translated a country and western song.') which, although true enough, smacked of a subtle bribery that I had thought Paco incapable of. Hiding my disappointment at my friend's underhand ways, I promised to translate Ms Gentry's 'Ode to Billie Joe' for next week, but will demand my pound of Valenciano flesh in return. (Revise ambiguous sentence.)

On informing Pamela of Francisco's ruse and the existence of yet another language to learn, she laughed heartily at the madman's brainwave, before telling me that she now quite often chatted to her friend Laura in Valenciano, but that Paco's wife also found conversation difficult to sustain. We lead parallel linguistic lives, but she always manages to stay one step ahead of me. Being in the presence of my wife reminded me that I have yet to invite the 'invitados' to her fast approaching birthday party, so I will now make out a comprehensive list.

Domingo, 12 de Octubre

I have much to report today as, until I had completed the onerous duty of contacting all of the invitees to Pamela's birthday party, I decided that I would not permit myself the pleasure of writing in my journal. I sincerely hope that, as well as the thousands of unknown future readers, my future grandchildren will also find my chronicle interesting, illuminating and instructive.

Needless to say, the potential co-creator of said descendants had not yet replied to my last email when I wrote him another one on Friday requesting his and Lena's presence on or before the 25th and assuring him, of course, that I would pay their air fares. I also asked him if he now had Herr Krankl fully introduced into his pocket - a disturbing image - and what advantages this was likely to produce. I refrained from employing those adjoining four letter words; 'paid' and 'work' in the email and my tact was rewarded by a speedy and informative, if still telegrammatic, reply which I will reproduce here:

Dear Mum and Dad,
Meant to write sooner but very busy. Herr Krankl deep in deepest pocket. Not forgotten Mum's birthday as Lena reminded me. No need to pay for tickets due to advance funds for business venture starting November. Will arrive evening 23rd and tell all then.
Alles Liebe,
Gerald

Rather than keeping their visit a surprise, I thought it more conducive to a happy home life to print out the email - after erasing 'as Lena reminded me' - and show it to my wife, who was delighted and asked me what we would be doing to celebrate our wedding anniversary. I told her that all celebrations on or around that date were well under control, which they weren't, but are now, up to a point.

After considering sending Uncle Harold and our friend Marcus emails in the hope that they would not see them until it was too late, I relented and, once Pamela was safely out of the house, first telephoned Uncle Harold, whose booming greeting of, "Ernest, old chap! How goes it!" made me fear that he had returned to the over-stimulated state of middle-aged, exercise-obsessed narcissism which Pamela had so cunningly cured him of. In this, however, I proved to be partially mistaken as, after beginning to dabble in general horticulture at his large home in the north of England, his fanatical disposition soon saw his mind zoom in to one particular area of plant life, and an especially fruitless one at that; the bonsai tree. He is now bonkers about bonsais and told me that he had already converted his indoor swimming pool into a greenhouse and was travelling far and wide in his quest for bonsai knowledge, culture and trees. "In fact," he bellowed, "I'm on a train to Osaka now." Japan! I had forgotten that mobile telephones could be used anywhere, so, resisting the impulse to hang up immediately, I nipped his bonsai ramblings in the bud and was quickly assured that he would be at Integración in time for his favourite niece's birthday.

Loath to make another expensive phone call, I emailed Marcus and approximately three minutes after clicking 'send' received a reply informing me that he would be *flying* to

Alicante on the 24th and would arrive here at approximately 6.45pm. He gave me no advice, guidance or suggestions in the email, so I trust that he remains cured of *his* addiction. I am sure two men of such similarly obsessive temperaments will not mind sharing a room.

With Integración thus fully booked, I was unable to invite Pamela's loathsome sister Sophie and her brats, or indeed her normal sister Joanne, so, as the rest of her relatives are far too decrepit to travel, I turned my attention to other prospective guests and at the time of writing have been assured of the presence of Alfredo and Marjorie, Trevor and Janice, Rocío and Pedro, Nerys and a maximum of half a dozen line dancers to be chosen at her discretion, the old crone at the shop who Pamela seems to be fond of, but who gave me her usual gimlet-eyed stare before realising whose husband I was, and, inevitably, Nora and Angeles. Paco and Laura are, of course, liaising directly with Andy and Ana regarding the bill of fare, for which I am extremely grateful, but hope that they don't exceed my theoretical budget, and Ana has been invited to invite all of the family members of her choice, bearing in mind that they will probably be doing most of the cooking.

The cooling weather made for a pleasant game of golf on Saturday and Alfredo remaining practically silent during the English-speaking back nine did wonders for my concentration, enabling me to get round in a more than acceptable ninety-two shots; my best score for months. Alfredo cutting out his grammar-free wittering, however, also improved *his* game and he beat me by three, so both of us entered the clubhouse in good spirits.

Remembering my new crusade to learn Valenciano, I took the proffered glass of beer and said, "Moltes gracies, Alfredo," to which he replied with a stunned silence. (Revise.) On explaining that I had decided that my integration process would never be complete without my learning the regional language, he shook his head and said that a man of my standing should concentrate on perfecting pure Castilian speech and forget about that vulgar language of the street. He explained that more refined people like ourselves always spoke Castellano and that he himself, although he could speak Valenciano perfectly, only employed it when dealing with wealthy local troglodytes who, although practically illiterate, were nevertheless lucrative clients.

I protested that, far from being refined, I was but a humble peasant farmer who wished to communicate with others of my ilk in their own language, at which he laughed and said that once a burgués (bourgeois) always a burgués, adding that while he thought it admirable that I dirtied my hands playing around with plants and chickens, my true status and my nationality meant that a Valenciano speaker would never feel comfortable addressing me in anything but Spanish.

My first impulse on hearing my noble endeavours disparaged in such a manner was to stand up and storm out of the clubhouse, until I remembered that we had come in Alfredo's car and also that I have far too few friends to quarrel with any of them. Sensing my displeasure, Alfredo laughed softly and, switching to English as was his curious habit when he wished to make a point, said, "Ernesto, you still lot not know about Spain. You must to trust me. This language thing like class divide. You one or you other and you can be only one." Switching mercifully back to Spanish, he appeased me somewhat by saying that despite all he had said, it was a good thing for me to understand Valenciano so that I would know when somebody was mocking or insulting me - something that I am almost sure never happens now - and that to say a few choice words from time to time would please people, but that if I insisted on speaking it all the time they would think me stranger than a green dog. I suppose I must trust Alfredo's native wisdom and the fact that he only has my own interests at heart, but I will first consult Paco, Andy, Trevor, and even Pamela, before I relinquish this facet of my integration process.

Today it has rained all day, so I have only been out to walk Sancho - on the lead - and later to take coffee in the clean bar for a change. The chattering ladies there were also speaking in Valenciano, so I bent an ear, figuratively speaking, to understand them, while ruing the fact that it is to be forbidden for me ever to speak it. On my return I observed Ernestina standing in the rain, as she has been all day, and was cheered by the thought that nobody can stop me speaking to my animals in Valenciano, which I will do from now on. Molt bé!

Martes, 14 de Octubre

Yesterday's 'advanced' class was, I think, terribly tiresome for all three participants as my relentless flashcard drilling bored Lola, who knows them all off by heart, bored me for the same reason, and almost killed Alfredo, whose brain appeared to have reached full capacity by twenty past seven, after which time he couldn't tell an umbrella from an aubergine. Unwilling to subject my liver to two almond liqueur evenings, I sent them both away with an 'adeu' to annoy Alfredo and sat down to put my figurative thinking cap on, before tearing it off my head in despair and going to seek Pamela's advice.

After informing her of the approximate state of affairs regarding the capabilities of all my students, she pointed out that advanced English classes, as far as she knew, were normally for students who had an almost native grasp of the language in both written and spoken form. "Half of the population of the British Isles," she said, "would find them hard going; especially the tabloid readers," before adding that beginners' English classes were for people who knew next to nothing. After pausing to let this sink in she seemed to become a little impatient and asked me what level my computer course classes were going to be. Having forgotten all about them, I racked my brains for the answer I had given her until she supplied me, rather suspiciously I thought, with, "Intermediate, I seem to recall." After pausing to let this sink in, she asked, "So what are your students, then?"

Brilliant! Intermediate is a wonderfully broad category and all of them fit into it one way or another, even Francisco, so from now on the Beginners will be promoted, and Lola and Alfredo will be demoted, to the new Intermediate Class and my Monday evenings will be free once more, or at least until I find a new batch of beginners. This is a great weight off my mind and also - although very much a secondary consideration - I will not be a penny worse off. My wife has great vision and can always be relied upon to give me a sterling second opinion on most subjects. I only wish she would avail herself of the opportunity to run things past me in a similar manner; something she seldom, if ever, does.

I decided to break the news of their downgrading to Lola and Alfredo immediately, in order to give them a full nine days to overcome their disappointment, but to my great surprise they were both more than happy - Alfredo seemed positively overjoyed - to join the others and said that they wouldn't miss this Wednesday's inaugural Intermediate Class for anything in the world, or words almost to that effect.

The benign rains having abated, this morning I carried out my final autumn planting of broccoli and sprouts, neglecting to plant leeks due to the slightly garlicky taste and their reminding me of Nerys, and I can now turn my attention to my future shed. This expensive investment in my plot reminded me of my decision to demand the sister's signature, but I must first decide how to approach this wily woman. My first impulse was to ask Pamela's advice, but no, I shall face this challenge alone and proudly present my wife with the signed papers to demonstrate yet again my ability to act decisively, something I need to remind her of from time to time.

I now address all my animals, including the chickens and turkeys, in Valenciano and they appear to understand me equally well - Ernestina rather better, if anything - and take no umbrage, something that could not be said for Nora, who greeted my 'Bon día' with an exquisitely enunciated 'Buenos días', before shuffling back into his house muttering under his breath. Delighted that my greeting made him use real words *and* disappear, he shall now join the animals in being addressed exclusively in that language. Pamela thinks this aversion to Valenciano is due to their families having only moved into the area in the last hundred years or so and says that she will also use this tactic when his wife next enters without knocking. Employed in this way, she said, Angeles would hopefully come to associate it with her own rudeness, like Pavlov's dogs - the language, I think she meant, not one of the dogs themselves.

Viernes, 17 de Octubre

On Wednesday evening at ten minutes to seven I wrote the words 'Intermediate Class' in large capital letters on the whiteboard which Pamela has recently purchased, before settling down to await my students' arrival. Paco appeared first and, on seeing the board, wheeled round as if to leave, before heeding my clap of the hands and following my pointed finger to his seat. No such effect - in fact no effect at all - did the happy news have on the other promoted students, who entered the room already speculating on Francisco's fate until I tapped the board sharply with a large knitting needle and said, "Intermediate students *always* speak English in class." When Lola and Alfredo arrived at five past as instructed, I introduced Alfredo - who they all knew - to the group and unsheathed my new 'Receptacles' flashcards, determined to launch the group in the manner in which they were to become accustomed.

For once, Francisco's arrival - interrupting Marta in mid 'flip top bottle' - caused only a minor interruption and he was able to avail us of the state of play in English. "In that meeting my work friends very with me," he said. "Cretin very angry and say he talk to *he* boss and me go fast. I think he have go not me. Now I put head down and do like cry when he come office. We see who win."

Suppressing a sigh as I remembered the words on the whiteboard, I picked up the cards and successfully taught them useful intermediate receptacle words such as hunting flask, attaché case, Fortnum and Mason hamper, saddlebag and milk crate; only stumbling over tupperware, which they insisted on pronouncing in Spanish - 'tuperwary' - until I had successfully deprogrammed them. I followed this up with a thorough revision of all the main tenses, to which everybody responded well expect Alfredo, whose fall from advanced student to intermediate class dunce does not seem to bother him in the slightest.

At eight o'clock I was faced with the dilemma of whether or not to invite Alfredo to my and Paco's little post-class soiree, but, remembering his aversion to Valenciano and uncertain of his stance on country music, I allowed him to leave with the others, before the two of us settled down to translate the rambling 'Ode to Billy Joe'. Paco was delighted with the song, which almost made him cry, but not quite so delighted by then being instructing to translate it back to me in Valenciano, which brought him even nearer to tears. I now know that black-eyed pea is 'guisante de ojo negro' in Spanish and 'pésol d'ull negre' in Valenciano; fascinating stuff which brings me ever nearer to trilingual status. On my asking him, Paco said that he couldn't think of a song that he wished me to translate for next week.

I spent all yesterday morning brushing up my computer skills in readiness for my first 'clase de informática' at night school. My fears over not knowing an Excel file from a 'cookie' I saw to be clearly unfounded the moment I walked through the classroom door and beheld the assembled studentry sitting rigidly before their computer screens as if they feared being swallowed up by them. Of those assorted townspeople - three men and four women - all appeared to be older than me apart from a scraggly young man who, rather than being the 'bohemian' I first took him for, turned out to be merely half-witted. My first impulse was to turn on my heels and flee, but, as I had already paid for the term, I took the only remaining seat - between the second oldest man and the drooling youth -

and decided to put down to experience whatever I was about to experience.

Of the others, none but one appeared to have touched a computer keyboard before, as was soon evident when the young, but far from attractive, female instructor told us to switch on the ancient machines. The previously silent women, all seated in the row in front of me, erupted simultaneously into guffaws, shrieks and whoops - especially whoops - of hilarity, the fattest of them begging the tutor to go easy on them as they were 'principiantes'. After our po-faced guide had switched on their computers and I had done the same for my neighbouring 'pensionista' and the twitching teenager, she invited us to grasp our mice and to practise moving the cursor around the screen, causing further uproar among the female contingent and tight-lipped concentration from the novice old boy. The other man, about Nora's age and just as rustic-looking, disobeyed instructions by opening a browser and beginning to quickly type in searches, while the poor simpleton ran his mouse repeatedly from chin to forehead and back again until I guided his sticky hand to the table top where it remained motionless.

After much hilarity in the first row, the teacher, satisfied that all had mastered the mouse except the youngster, showed us how to open the browser and told us to type in something of interest to us. As my impassive neighbour had slowly typed in 'albaricoque' (apricot), I showed solidarity by choosing 'alcachofa' (artichoke), while the women whooped, the boy picked his nose, and the other old man typed furiously on a page that appeared to contain images of scantily clad females. The teacher then informed us that we had just discovered the magic of the internet, which would enable us to find information about all sorts of things from all over the world, and suggested that we spend a while 'surfeando' the net until we got the hang of it.

While the women cackled and hooted over the doings of sundry celebrities and my neighbour snorted in disgust over new-fangled cultivation methods, the teacher prised the boy's hand from his mouse and found him a computer game which he then played with astonishing speed and skill, suggesting to me that he may be one of those prodigies trapped in a fool's body whom one sometimes reads about. Meanwhile, the aging libertine clicked and typed furiously until his mobile telephone rang and he scuttled out of the room to answer it, causing my neighbour to turn to me and whisper hoarsely, "Es un gran putero." I nodded sagely, before quickly typing in the words 'putero English translation' and finding that it means whoremonger. I found this most shocking as I am sure that prostitution is just as illegal in Spain as in England, and also due to the man's advanced age. I will consult my Spanish friends about this disturbing news, NOT, I may add, due to any personal interest in the sordid business, but merely to discover what the male population may or may not be getting up to.

After twenty minutes of surfing, our grim-faced instructress showed us how to open a document, which nobody found very interesting, before telling us that next week she would introduce us to the wonderful world of emails. I stayed behind after the others had shuffled, wobbled and loped out of the classroom and expressed my concern that the class was too easy and that the 'grupo intermediato' would be more suitable for me. At this she laughed - a pleasant laugh which made me feel that she was a pretty woman trapped behind an ugly face - and said that this was the beginners, intermediate and advanced group all rolled into one. The beginners, she said, changed every year but normally comprised of similarly silly women and taciturn men, while the 'hombre verde' (green man) used his intermediate skills in the same way every year, preferring to use the school's computers to the one he shared with his grandchildren. The young man, it transpired, far from being a half-wit, had an IQ of 155 which only manifested itself when subjected to certain stimuli, including complex computer games.

This will teach me to be judgemental - something I am rarely guilty of - as the young man I pitied is worthy of respect and the future reader will see that I am not above admitting to my faults by the fact that I have faithfully recorded my initial impression of him, rather than pretending that I recognised his genius all along. By contrast, the respectable-looking elder is in fact a lecherous, depraved, degenerate exploiter of womankind. I will ask my Spanish friends if they know any green men in order to gauge their reaction, before broaching the general subject of sleaze in Spain. All I can say is that the old green man must be like a green dog to get up to those disgusting capers at his age, which should make sense to the attentive future reader.

On asking the teacher if there were another course which I could switch to, she suggested that one of the English groups may be of interest to me. My initial delight at being taken for a native was lessened considerably when, on cheerfully explaining that I was in fact English, she apologised and said that she thought I was German. Before Gerald met Lena this aspersion would have caused me mortal offence, but as my opinion of our former foes has risen somewhat since then, I accepted her slanderous statement quite calmly and have since appeased myself by the fact that she could not pin my very faintly foreign accent down to my former country. It is also true that the Germans I have seen in Spain do seem slightly more linguistically gifted than the lamentably monolingual British expats. At least when they call rudely for a tankard of beer they usually do so in Spanish.

So, unless I want to do cross-stitching, pottery in the presence of Nerys, or flop about in a leotard in yoga class, I am stumped. On asking if I would be able to ask for a refund, she said that it was an administrative matter, which I took to mean no, so I may attend some future classes merely out of sociological interest, unless I can make friends with the grumpy apricot man.

Lunes, 20 de Octubre

This weekend was to have been a quiet one, all the better to ready myself for the whirlwind of Pamela's birthday and anniversary celebrations which will soon be upon us, but unexpected events made it into a traumatic, but ultimately... well, I will explain.

As Alfredo was unable to play golf on Saturday, I decided to fill this gap in my busy schedule by seeking out the elusive sister. Having visited the town hall on Friday, I went armed with the necessary papers, my passport and identity card, a pen, and a clipboard, in the hope of securing a doorstep signature before she had time to think of an excuse not to sign. In order to appear businesslike and even less foreign-looking than usual, I wore a jacket, tie, and stout shoes with which to prevent the door being slammed in my face. Thus equipped, I rapped her knocker and was pleased to hear a shuffle of feet and the click of a lock, before her grizzled head appeared in an aperture just wide enough in which to insert my size ten foot. I flashed my 'carné de identidad' before explaining rapidly and clearly who I was and what I required, at which her wary expression melted into a smile and she said, "Un momento, por favor," before leaving me on the doorstep, clipboard in hand. I extracted my foot and waited with much anticipation for her return, but the moment became a minute, then five, and I began to feel rather self-conscious standing there before the open door.

Imagine my astonishment when I turned to see a group of neighbours standing three or four houses down the street observing me, with the sister among them. Before I had time to approach her, a police car screeched to a halt and two young 'policias locales' sprang out and moved towards me cautiously in what looked very much like a pincer movement. Feeling that my British passport might carry more weight than the flimsy ID card, I held it aloft and truly believe that this prevented the handcuffs that one of the officers brandished being slipped onto my wrists. I quickly explained the reason for my visit and showed my would be captors the contents of my clipboard, before pointing down the street to where the sister *had* been standing, for now there was nobody in sight. One of the officers knocked on the door and, receiving no reply, closed it, before exchanging words with the other 'cop' to the effect that the woman, who shopped at his mother's bakery, appeared to be 'volviéndose loca' (going crazy) since her return from South America, which in that family was no surprise. He went on to advise me to get in touch with the woman's niece - an old school friend of his - who might be able to talk some sense into her, before kindly finding me her number on his mobile telephone.

I drove back to the village in a state of considerable agitation and immediately relayed to Pamela the story of my ordeal and my fears that hereditary loopiness may prevent me from ever actually owning the ground under Ernestina's feet. Once she had stopped laughing, she took the clipboard from me and told me that she would attend to the matter today, before making me a cup of tea. While drinking the soothing cuppa I insisted that I was more than capable of fighting my own land battles, to which she replied, "Yes, but the sister is a woman and I presume the niece is a woman too, so a woman's touch may be what is required here. Now go and take Sancho for a nice relaxing walk." So that is what I did, if the company of a stick-obsessed dog can be said to be relaxing, and when I came back she had gone.

Imagine my surprise when she returned an hour later with the sister's signature on the dotted line! Pamela had, she said, simply phoned the niece and arranged to meet at her aunt's house, where the niece had told her to sign the silly paper for the nice lady, which she did without demur. "It was easy," Pamela said, "because the niece is a lovely woman. She's called Marta and she comes to your class."

Aargh! The future reader will excuse my uncharacteristic use of informal English, but this is the only word which can describe my reaction to the news that the niece was Marta and that, had I simply rung the number... but, no matter, the plot is now officially mine - and Pamela's, of course - and I can finally open negotiations for the purchase of some or all of Pedro and Rocío's long neglected land in order to expand my farming project.

Despite my annoyance at not 'doing the deeds deed' myself, I was most grateful for Pamela's speedy action and this reminded me that I have not yet bought her a birthday and anniversary present - traditionally a single item for convenience - and that I should have put my gift-giving thinking cap on earlier as it is now too late to avail myself of the vast internet shopping emporium. As I believe it is our silver wedding anniversary, something made of that metal would be appropriate and I will see what the town jeweller's has to offer tomorrow.

Jueves, 23 de Octubre

As Gerald and Lena are due to arrive this evening, I shall get my journal up to date before the torrent of news which I expect the forthcoming days to bring. Last night's class was mercifully uneventful as Francisco's future job prospects are still in limbo, although he is quietly confident that his nemesis will shortly be vacating his office and returning to Madrid or wherever they send him next. Former advanced student Alfredo is still struggling to catch up with the former beginner students, but now appears to accept that there is little future in grammarless English and has knuckled down to flashcard repetition as obediently as the rest of them. I thanked Marta for her assistance in securing her mad relative's signature and found myself inviting her and Jorge to Pamela's birthday party on Saturday. After that, of course, I also had to invite Lola and, with great misgivings, Francisco, which means four more mouths to feed and the additional anxiety of that crackpot's unpredictable behaviour, although there are plenty of goats for him to talk to on Andy's finca.

Pamela had not overlooked the fact, as I had, that the spare room - for the other spare room is now officially 'Gerald and Lena's room' - contains only a double bed, and she has had the foresight to borrow a camp bed from Nerys which she hopes that her more nimble uncle will be happy to sleep on. I would have been more than happy to let Uncle Harold and Marcus fight over the duvet.

Viernes, 24 de Octubre

Today I am making another unaccustomed post-lunch journal entry to report the arrival of Gerald and the delightful Lena yesterday evening in a hire car. In a hire car because, it appears, money is now no object due to the guaranteed prospects of my son's first ever commercial venture which has yet to commence. As a man of considerable experience in business matters, I urged caution regarding unnecessary expenditure - especially of Herr Krankl's money - before asking him to tell me all about this exciting new project.

It transpires that Gerald has ingratiated himself with the Krankl's to such an extent that, after diplomatically declining to join Lena's father in the delicatessen trade, he has convinced him that with a little backing he could successfully represent German alternative energy companies in Spain where, he told him, there was plenty of sun but little business acumen. "And where," I asked him, "did you acquire *your* business acumen all of a sudden?" "I can turn my hand to anything, Dad," he replied, "and take a look at this, and this," before producing a photograph of himself dressed in a suit which, with his revolting ponytail out of sight, made him look like the ideal son, and a business card. The card read, 'Gerald Postlethwaite, BSc (Hons) Renewable Energy Solutions for Off-grid Applications' with an attractive green logotype, designed by Lena, and the Krankl's impressive-sounding address as his headquarters.

While gratified by these developments, I pointed out that he was, as yet, no linguist and had not, in fact, finished his degree. He laughed off these minor matters and said that all of the Germans he was likely to deal with spoke good English and that he was already studying Spanish and intended to practise as much as possible during the week they were to stay with us. I shook my head and said that he would find Spanish a jolly sight more difficult to master than he thought, to which he replied, "Ya veremos, padre," so we shall indeed see. The degree, he said, he had awarded to himself for the considerable knowledge of green energy that he had accumulated over the years and that, in any case, nobody was likely to check up. At this point a mobile telephone rang and Gerald produced a slim device from his waistcoat pocket and answered, "Gutten abend... Heinrich, how goes it, man? Einen moment while I find a quiet spot," before leaving the room to allow his alter ego to natter on to Heinrich in tones reminiscent of fake City of London joviality for a quarter of an hour. So far, it must be said, so good.

Now I shall sheath my ballpoint - for I have yet to buy new cartridges for my elegant fountain pen - and enjoy my last hours of peace before Uncle Harold and Marcus arrive to fill Intergración to capacity. I shall be glad when the next forty-eight hours are over and I can return to the agrarian peace to which I am striving to become accustomed.

I feel that an urgent journal entry is in order before the birthday celebrations commence and the remarkable events of yesterday evening begin to lose their delightful freshness in my mind. Uncle Harold arrived first in a large hire car, followed shortly afterwards by Marcus in a smaller hire car, so it is fortunate that Nora and Angeles are too old to own a car and that all of Rocío and Pedro's vehicles are rusting on their plot, or there would have been nowhere to park them.

Uncle Harold has changed insomuch as he now wears normal clothes and has gained just enough weight so that his veins no longer look like they are about to explode, but, other than that, he remains his old enthusiastic self, save that he now booms on about bonsais instead of fitness. After being introduced to our future daughter-in-law, hugging his niece in a most unavuncular way, and crushing my hand marginally less than in June, he scuttled back out to his car and returned with a bonsai tree which he said was just a taster and *not* Pamela's birthday present. "That," he said, "or rather those, will be delivered sometime next week," so I shudder to think how many of the useless, stunted little insults to the plant kingdom will soon be littering my patio.

Uncle Harold had hardly settled into his monothematic monologue before he was cut short by the arrival of our other guest. Marcus greeted us all cheerfully and said that he felt that he was finally overcoming his fear of flying, before lapsing into silence and only speaking when prompted to join the conversation, which was mostly about bonsais. When Uncle Harold went to the bathroom, freeing up the oxygen for the use of others, Pamela remarked to Marcus that he seemed rather subdued and appeared to have lost weight. The previously unstoppable mouth of our friend opened, closed, and opened again to say, "Well, the advice that you gave me, Ernest, about not constantly giving advice seems to have worked *too* well. My becoming a good listener again appeared to please people so much and make them seem to like me so much more that I found myself behaving in the same way at work. As my job is to give advice and guidance, people became rather dissatisfied when I asked them *their* opinion on the best way to resolve their problems, and my colleagues and assistants have begun to treat me with positive contempt. Try as I may, I can't seem to go back to my old ways at all. I'm at my wit's end and I hoped that you two might be able to offer me some suggestions."

At this point Uncle Harold thundered down the stairs with an armful of bonsai books, so Marcus went to freshen up while my wife and I feigned interest in indoor and outdoor bonsais, small, smaller and tiny bonsais, rare and priceless bonsais and suchlike, until a glance at my wife told me that her mind was chugging away and about to come up with one of her ideas.

"Harold," she interjected, "you'll be alright on the camp bed, won't you?" to which he replied, "Of course, after practically sleeping on the floor in Japan, I'll find it quite comfortable," before launching into an account of his far-eastern bonsai tour which Pamela, on hearing Marcus descending the stairs, interrupted to suggest that he go and unpack as dinner would soon be ready.

"Marcus," she said when Uncle Harold had gone, "you used to pride yourself on having a photographic memory, didn't you?" "Ah, in my old arrogant days I might have said such a thing," he replied, "but it is true that I have a certain capacity for retaining information, yes." "Good," she said, "go to the computer and learn everything you can about bonsai trees in the next twenty minutes, then come into the kitchen for your instructions while I am dishing out the dinner."

Marcus obeyed, Harold reappeared, and their ensued one of the most entertaining dinners I have experienced during my time in Spain, or indeed in my whole life. Over the soup, Marcus interrupted Uncle Harold to question him regarding the origins of bonsai cultivation, before arguing vehemently that the Chinese rather than the Japanese were the true pioneers, supporting his opinion with an impressive array of facts, figures and dates. After pausing to congratulate Pamela on her delicious lamb casserole, Marcus then quizzed Uncle Harold regarding his pruning, trimming, clamping, grafting and wiring methods, before finding fault with everything he said and making alternative suggestions. By the time the plum pudding - alas not yet plums from my own trees - was served, Marcus was thoroughly enjoying being his old self again, while Uncle Harold had wilted into a state reminiscent of the days when Pamela had tranquilised him into submission, and, after pleading jetlag, soon asked to be excused, thus allowing the five of us to enjoy coffee in a peace only punctuated by our strenuous efforts to stifle our laughter.

After another fact-absorbing twenty minutes at the computer, Marcus bade us goodnight and went to his room where, he told us this morning, his comments on the disastrous effects on bonsai cultivation of the 1923 Tokyo earthquake were met with silence. Indeed, it was in near silence that breakfast was eaten this morning, as every time Uncle Harold appeared likely to open his mouth to speak, Marcus's gleaming eyes were upon him like a fox's at the door of a chicken coop. I should not think they will spend much time together at today's party.

Domingo, 26 de Octubre

Our two guests spent no time at all together at yesterday's splendid birthday party, but the mere presence of Marcus within fifty yards of him kept Uncle Harold off the subject of bonsais, especially after Andy had called them 'a fecking pointless waste of tree', which offended Nerys who has two.

As the sun was shining, the guests mingled on the patio and I made all the pertinent introductions, saddling Nora and Angeles with the old crone, Esme, who was still unable or unwilling to look me in the eye, and telling Francisco - all smiles in his checked shirt and bowtie - where the goats lived. While the lovely Ana directed a bevy of female relatives in the kitchen, Gerald soon cornered Andy, before leading him away from the house, pointing to the roof, and signalling where, I presume, his solar panels ought to go. I determined to tell him off later for talking business to our host, before turning to greet Rocío and Pedro and speaking to them of my progress on the plot. As expected, their glazed eyes - especially Pedro's - indicated their limited interest in horticultural matters and I said that it was such a pity not to exploit the rich soil hidden underneath all the old vehicles on their land. Pedro replied that the need to care for his guitarist's fingernails prevented him from carrying out manual tasks such as gardening, but that Rocío's cousin had promised to take all the scrap away at some time in the near future. As I suspected that an artistic gypsy's idea of the near future and mine differed considerably, I told them that I knew of a 'chatarrero' (scrap metal dealer) who would pay an excellent price for all that valuable metal. Spotting an avaricious sparkle in Rocío's eyes, I went on to visualise for their benefit the beauty of a paved patio area of approximately twenty square metres - surrounded by a nice high fence which would give them privacy and splendid acoustics for open air rehearsals - which the proceeds of the scrap would enable them to have built. Feeling that I had said enough for the time being and not yet wishing to broach the subject of how they might dispose of the superfluous portion of their land, I left the seed of my idea to germinate in their brains and went to join Gerald and Andy.

I found Gerald busy bewitching Andy with facts and figures regarding solar panels and wind turbines, so, as lunch was about to be served, I prised my son away and beseeched him not to talk shop on such a celebratory occasion. He acquiesced, saying that the perfect orientation of the roof had made him forget himself, before asking to be introduced to a group of people who could only have been the line dancers. It was with these gawky foreigners that he sat at lunch, producing much laughter from their end of the table and concluding in a distribution of business cards and mutual promises to be in touch very soon. Three months ago he would have had them subscribing to save a rainforest or protect the polar icecap, but such is his versatility that I expect their houses will soon be festooned with ugly solar panelling, something which will not be happening to the more rustic roofscape of Integración and adjoining properties, I hope.

While Gerald was bamboozling the naïve expats, Lena sat up near the head of the table with Pamela, myself and other close friends, with the exception of Francisco, who had somehow contrived to slot himself between her and Paco's wife Laura. Alfredo was seated to my left and appeared to be in very good spirits right from the start of the delicious meal, which included numerous vegetarian options thanks to Ana's sterling efforts. On asking him why he was so cheerful, he replied that the latest financial news augured so well for his business that he might have to take on extra staff. Pleased by this, I asked him if the economy was making an unexpected recovery, to which he replied that I had evidently not seen the news. "Big crash," he said, "all over world yesterday. Stock markets down muchísimo. Spain economy now sure caput and lot of bankrupt soon come cry to me."

This was not something I wished to hear on a day of such merriment, although it only affects me insomuch as the hypothetical sale of Integración would probably soon fetch little more than the price of a double garage on the commuter belt, so I put it out of my mind and turned my attention to the rest of the guests. Marcus having seated himself next to Pamela, Uncle Harold had joined the line dancers at the other end of the table where Gerald's amusing solar power patter forced him to keep his bonsai fetish under a bushel until, after the meal, he found a sympathetic listener in Nerys. They seemed to get on like a small tree on fire and perhaps they ought to marry, as I doubt that anybody else would have either of them, if that makes sense.

After coffee and the subsequent serving of a rather refined 'cava' of my choosing, I presented Pamela with a solid silver carriage clock which she thanked me for with a hug and a peck on the cheek, having the diplomacy not to mention - until this morning - that the traditional gift for a thirtieth anniversary was, in fact, pearl, or pearls. After my irrelevant offering, she received further gifts from our guests, ranging from a tasteful leather travel bag from Marcus, through a pair of rhinestone-studded line dancing bootstraps from Trevor and Janice, to a slightly soiled Charles and Diana mug filled with roasted almonds from Angeles and Nora. Francisco, who had been making love - in the Victorian sense - to Lena throughout the meal, saved his offering of a wooden back-scratcher cum metric ruler until last and amused us all with a vivid demonstration of its uses, before inviting Lena to visit the goats' house. Fortunately for me - and for her - she chose to stay by my side as I congratulated Ana, her mother, her deaf cousin Beatriz, and sundry other assistants on their excellent cooking, promising that Pamela and I would do the same for them whenever required, which I trust their culinary pride will never permit. On asking after Uncle Arsenio, who had disappeared midway through dessert, Ana said that he had been sent to scrub the pans in order to aid his digestion, and would be allowed out again when the greater part of the cava had been consumed.

Shortly afterwards the old crone addressed my directly for the first time ever, saying simply, "Huevos," before averting her eyes and chomping her gums. As the word for eggs in Spanish is also employed in the way that less refined English speakers say 'bollocks', I was unsure how to react, until Pamela explained that Esme would be happy to buy our surplus eggs from us. "To suck them?" I responded wittily to my wife, before my cheerful nod and thumbs up to the bizarre woman sent her scuttling back to her peer group; namely Nora and Angeles.

At this point Rocío and Pedro regaled us with a similar selection of popular songs as at my birthday party, which prompted the line dancers to perform an absurd little jig in which Francisco joined rather energetically, inventing novel dance steps which Trevor would have done well to document.

Shortly afterwards I led Francisco aside and told him that the line dancers met every Tuesday morning and that, if he were ever free at that time, they would raise their cowboy hats and welcome him with open arms. After mischievously planting this seed in his addled brain, I strolled over to where Trevor, Janice, Gerald and Marcus were discussing the dreaded topic of central heating, just in time to hear our guest contradicting Gerald regarding the efficiency of solar energy. On raising my eyebrows, Marcus smiled and said, "Don't worry, Ernest, I have it under control. I can turn my advice tap off whenever I wish," before wistfully scanning the patio in search of Uncle Harold, who appeared still to be under the spell of Nerys's singsong chatter.

I could go on, but, loath to subject the future reader to irrelevant gossip, I shall close my journal on yet another felicitous Spanish celebration; each one a far cry from the humdrum golf club shindigs which formed the highlight of my monotonous social life during my erstwhile drab existence. The only grey lining to an otherwise silver cloud (revise) was the slip of paper which Andy popped into my shirt pocket as we said our goodbyes. The cost of the food and drink was not low, but I consoled myself with the fact that for little more than the cost of lunch for two in Lorca I had fed the five thousand, figuratively speaking.

Martes, 28 de Octubre

Yesterday being the day of our *pearl* wedding anniversary, symbolised by the mint imperial which Pamela has jokingly placed atop the solid silver clock which now adorns the mantelpiece, I felt that yet another feast was called for, but, unwilling to drain the coffers any more than was strictly necessary, I decided that lunch at Paco's brother-in-law's restaurant would be the best option for our party of six. After taking our seats at the table on the patio, I recommended the excellent 'menú del día' very strongly indeed, but needn't have worried as the owner Pepe, on clapping eyes on Gerald and being informed by him that it was our 'Bodas de Perla', said that it would be his personal pleasure to make us the best vegetarian paella that we had ever tasted. Gerald begged leave to be present at the creation of this dish and scuttled away after Pepe with a solar-powered glint in his eye.

Left to our own devices, conversation was rather stilted until Marcus proved that he can indeed regulate the flow of his advice nozzle by drawing Uncle Harold into conversation regarding Saturday's knees up. That man, cautiously at first, praised the food and the setting until, when it became clear that he was to be allowed to express his opinions unchallenged, he touched upon the subject of the guests. "The Welsh lady, Nerys, is a most charming person. We share many interests, including... we share many interests and I would rather like to see her again." Pamela was quick to produce a mobile telephone which I did not know she possessed and suggest that Uncle Harold call her and invite her to join us for coffee, which he did.

Gerald, meanwhile, had clearly not stood looking idly over the cook's shoulder, for when he and Pepe eventually emerged with the steaming 'paellera' and placed it on the table, they walked over to the roadside from where Gerald explained how the sun's rays would make a beeline for his soon to be shiny roof and make electricity bills a thing of the past. Pepe, apparently convinced by my son's extraordinarily swift calculations, took the notes that he had quickly scribbled and returned inside, leaving us to enjoy a dish every bit as delicious as he had promised, despite the absence of meat or fish. At this point Gerald began to question Uncle Harold about his large property in Northern England and if it were not very windy up there, until his mother laid down her fork, crossed her arms, and gave our son her famous - to me - questioning look that admitted of only one response; in this case an immediate end to his business spiel. I am not sure if I don't prefer the anti-materialistic Gerald of old to this implacable sales demon, but at least his future success will make the hypothetical purchase of Nora and Angeles's house less likely to be a burden on Herr Krankl and myself.

While on the subject of my son's future happiness, I feel that Lena would feature far more in this journal if it contained visual images, as it has dawned on me that she makes little contribution to our interesting conversations and that she seems just as happy with Gerald's new venture as with his old unproductive ways and equally as uninvolved. I am not an expert on womankind, but I do know that she is either very deep or very shallow and I shall have to ask Pamela, who is bound to know, which is the case. Nerys, on the other hand, who joined us remarkably quickly, is clearly neither very deep nor entirely shallow, as, in the presence of a male admirer - and a very wealthy one to boot - she modified her usual tittle-tattle and was able to draw him out on the subjects of his travels, his lifestyle, his taste in home furnishing - on every subject, in fact, except bonsai trees. Hopefully when they marry they will go to live at his house in England, where I am sure they would be happier than here, and much further away.

Although the lunch proved to be not entirely without outgoings from my much depleted wallet, it was a pleasant one and a fitting finale to a successful celebratory weekend. Now that Uncle Harold and Marcus have finally left, I shall be glad to spend the rest of the week with my nuclear family and tomorrow morning will use my own considerable powers of persuasion to enlist Gerald's assistance regarding the pressing matter of the foundations for the shed.

Jueves, 30 de Octubre

Today I have much to report, as has usually been the case in this turbulent final month of my first year in Spain. Had I kept a journal during my former life, it would have been a far more mundane and less enthralling affair than this colourful and kaleidoscopic composition in which the lives of many fascinating individuals intertwine before the future readers' eyes. (A fine sentence, including rather good alliteration.)

After breakfast yesterday, and before I had time to corner him, Gerald left the house and since then has only been present at mealtimes, if then. He is, he says, maximising his Spanish learning time by visiting all the bars, restaurants and shops in La Puebla and Villeda and, just occasionally, bringing up the subject of alternative energy. In this latter respect, he says, he has found the expat community to be far more receptive; partly due to the absence of linguistic barriers, but mostly because of their astonishing gullibility. He has already received several serious expressions of interest and, on his return to Germany, will begin to give exact quotes. Lena has accompanied him faithfully on all occasions except to the dirty bar, which she found too intimidating and filthy to enter, and her beguiling presence can only have increased his kudos, as will the fact that they both eschewed their 'hippie' garb in favour of civilian clothes.

Thus my desire to enlist his expertise and muscle in the arduous task of laying down the shed foundations has remained unspoken, and far be it for me to hold my son back from taking his long delayed first step up the ladder to financial security. I shall ask him to at least write down detailed instructions before he leaves and I am quietly confident of being able to hoodwink Nora into doing a good deal of the spadework by feigning an incompetence that I no longer wholly possess, as I now know one end of a spade, and azada, from the other only too well.

Despite the plot's continuing shedlessness, however, it is now an even greater pleasure to potter around it as I feed the birds and Ernestina, pick a few weeds, survey my shoots, or smell my composter, because it is now legally *mine* and feels somehow different underfoot; almost an extension of myself, in fact. After all, does the land belong to me or do I belong to the land? As my wisdom increases with age, I may one day be able to answer this, and other, profound questions.

Philosophical aside over, I must plunge the reader back into the tiresome saga of Francisco's workplace struggles which have done so much to curtail the development of my teaching methodology, including my long neglected Singing English experiments and other ideas which will no doubt emerge when my mind is free of these irrelevant digressions. Francisco arrived at ten minutes to seven while I was writing interrogatives on the whiteboard and I first became aware of his presence when he whispered, "Ernesto, I no job," in my ear from a distance of approximately six inches, causing me to jump out of my skin, figuratively speaking, and send the whiteboard crashing to the floor. He apologised, straightened my spectacles, righted the board, and went on to say that he did not wish the others to know that he had lost his job, before tapping his nose, winking twice, and taking his seat.

When Marta and Jorge arrived shortly afterwards, he greeted them with unusual elation, asked them if they had had a good day and, without waiting for a reply, went on to say, "My day good too. *Very* busy and lot of work, but happy day." He greeted the others with similarly verbless effusions of workplace joy, before we settled down to revise our receptacle vocabulary. The class proved to be the most industrious for many weeks, despite Francisco's continual nose-tapping and winking, and by eliminating any unnecessary free speech we reached eight o'clock without a single reference being made to his job.

On opening the almond liqueur, Paco said that he would try to help Francisco find a new one. On asking him what he would help him to find, he said that it was patently obvious that he had lost his job and that it was imperative to get him back behind a desk a quickly as possible, as only with his mind occupied would he avoid plunging into the 'abismo' of lunacy once more, which, he warned, was as likely to occur in our class as anywhere else. Alarmed by this prospect, I put my thinking cap on and soon recalled that Alfredo had mentioned that he might need to take on more staff and also that Francisco's first taste of Line Dancing suggested that this activity could be of therapeutic benefit to him, if not to the other participants. Paco agreed to call on him before the end of the week and tell him that he need not hide his disappointment from his supportive classmates and that Line Dancing classes at the Casa de Cultura commenced at ten o'clock every Tuesday. I saw no need to relay any of this information to Pamela.

Sábado, 1 de NOVIEMBRE 2008

Un año! Yes, my first year in Spain has now concluded and I feel that I have taken gigantic strides towards my integration into this rustic community. My Spanish, although not as good as Pamela's, has come on leaps and bounds this summer and I now understand everything which is said to me, or about me, and can make myself understood perfectly well, albeit without the vast range of vocabulary which I possess in English or a complete understanding of the annoying and unnecessary subjunctive tense. This achievement, along with my smattering of Valenciano, must put me among the top ten percent of inland foreigners, linguistically speaking, and if we include the thousands of beer-swilling, sun-worshipping coastal heathens, perhaps the top two percent; quite an achievement for a man approaching the autumn of his life and who just one year ago didn't know an alcachofa from an alpargata (espadrille).

I must not, however, rest on my laurels and I am determined that my second year will be one of *consolidation* in all facets of my life here, in approximately this order: language, friendships, horticulture, animal management, land expansion, culture, travel and golf. One year from now when I re-read today's journal entry, I shall go through that list and measure my progress. Charles Darwin once said that he who wastes one hour does not know the value of life, or words to that effect, and I shall not be that person as even my golf outings have their purpose; namely exercise and Spanish conversation, the game itself being of secondary, or even tertiary, importance.

Gerald and Lena left for the airport this afternoon, my son

well satisfied with the interest he has generated in his products, although he told us that the locals have expressed very little interest in 'green' energy. The expats, by contrast, are much more enthusiastic, some even being eager to heat their swimming pools by solar means, which Gerald thinks lamentably bourgeois, but potentially very profitable. From now on he will have to lead a dual existence, donning his silly waistcoat and ideas only at the weekend. This metamorphosis is, I feel, due in no small degree to my subtly persuasive influence which has finally seeped into his brain, although Pamela says that it is *despite* this, which seems to be an odd application of female logic, but no matter.

My son did eventually find the time to write down detailed instruction regarding the construction of the shed foundations and, once I have decided exactly where it is to go and know the exact dimensions of my shed, I shall throw myself into the task with my usual enthusiasm. He recommended the use of metal to strengthen the concrete, citing iron rods and golf clubs as ideal for the purpose, and I am sure that a perusal of Pedro's junkyard will supply enough metallic matter to cut down the amount of concrete mixing considerably. I must not, however, rush into this project and later kick myself for placing the shed in the wrong place, especially if I take into account the new layout of the plot once the greater part of Pedro and Rocío's land has been incorporated. Nor must I lose sight of the fact that Nora and Angeles could depart this world at any moment, although probably not simultaneously, and make their land available for further expansion. No, I must certainly give this shed business a good deal of thought before I commence.

Today the first non-white president of America has been elected, which is excellent news for all non-racist people, amongst whom I include myself now that my aversion to Germans has been removed by the lovely Lena, and the fact that German blood may well soon be coursing through the veins of the next generation of Postlethwaites. Besides, the royal family has a good deal of it and they are never rude to waiters. Good for Obama, I say, and I sincerely hope that he does a good job and that nobody shoots him.

Pamela arrived home from Line Dancing today with her new mobile telephone stuck to her ear and into which she was imparting some very stern English words, immediately making me suspect that Francisco had indeed attended the dancing and that the consequences had not been wholly favourable. I need not have feared, however, as once she had switched the silly device off, she told me two pieces of good news, the first of which was that Francisco's Line Dancing debut had been a success and that he had been rapidly taken under the collective wing of several of the ladies. This attention, Pamela said, made him positively glow, but she is well aware that this glow must be carefully regulated to avoid it turning into flashing lights, metaphorically speaking, so she has apprised Trevor, Janice and Nerys of the brittle nature of his brain cells - my words, not hers - and they will monitor his mental state each week.

The second piece of news was even better and pertained to Pamela's conversation on her mobile telephone, which it transpires that she bought a fortnight ago, but hadn't deemed necessary to tell me about. The recipient of her wrath was an English central heating 'engineer' - he probably picked up his certificates from the air hostess on the flight over - who has now backed out of the installation he was due to commence this month, citing difficulties with supplies. That the man was recommended by Nerys came as no surprise to me and I chose that moment - the wrong one, it turned out - to express my surprise that we were not going to become Gerald's first customers and cover the roof of Integración with ugly plaques.

"We're not talking about making a slice of toast," she snapped, "we're talking about keeping this big old place warm this winter with *proper* central heating," before jabbing at her device and ringing Andy, who I had thought was mainly my friend, and asking him to recommend a thoroughly professional Spanish company, whatever the cost. My severe shock on hearing this last statement was somewhat assuaged by the fact that Andy doubts that the company he recommends will be able to do the job at short notice, so if my luck holds I may have one more winter in which to convince my wife that central heating is unnecessary. Even while writing these last words, however, I know deep down that Pamela will 'salir con la suya' (get her way) and must console myself with the fact that I shan't have to clean and replenish the wood burning stove every single day and that our roof will remain free from unaesthetic foreign bodies.

Jueves, 6 de Noviembre

Francisco's quiet tap on the classroom door at five past seven yesterday evening made us all prepare our best expressions of sympathy, but his entrance in cowboy hat and neckerchief, his little jig as he approached his chair, and a lithely executed full turn before sitting down, made it clear that commiserations could be dispensed with. Cutting short my explanation of how we celebrate the fifth of November in England by burning the effigy of the evil ringleader of a band of murderous papists, I reluctantly asked him if he had enjoyed his first Line Dancing session.

"It fantastic, Ernesto," he said. "Now I not worry about no job. Now I practise steps with video all day. Cowboy boots and chaleco (waistcoat) come in post soon. I very happy." Seeing Lola's mouth opening, I swept up my 'Freshwater Fish' cards and compelled her to say bream, perch and trout rather than dispense the sage advice which was upon her lips, and from that moment on I kept up a relentless stream of flashcards which soon silenced even Francisco's humming of 'Achy Breaky Heart' and heated his head sufficiently to make him take his ridiculous hat off. At five to eight I put down my 'English Counties' cards and said, "Now we can speak, but only in English." Their minds mangled by their futile efforts to pronounce Leicestershire, Worcestershire and Warwickshire, only Lola was able to respond to my kind invitation, saying, "But Francisco, line dancing is fine and I know that your mother will enjoy having you at home, for a while, but you must really think about getting another job," to which he replied, "No more office. I will be line dancer professional and travel all over world."

I have nothing more to add on this subject which has already filled a disproportionate number of journal pages and may be giving the future reader the impression that my life consists of nothing but trivialities. Indeed, when I returned upstairs with the almond liqueur, I begged Paco to make no further comment on this latest turn of events in the potty man's life and instead decided to question him regarding the surprising comment made by the old man at the computer class about the even older and reputedly 'green' man. Fearing a guarded response to my enquiries, I asked him straight off if he himself was a 'putero', an accusation which he denied much more strongly than I had expected him to.

I said that I was joking and knew full well that a staunch family man like himself would have nothing to do with such sordid proceedings, but went on to ask him where this supposed whoring took place. He said that it took place, he believed, largely in the clubs, but that he was really the wrong person to ask as it had been many years since he had set foot in such a place. On asking him where these dens of vice were hidden, he laughed and asked me if I had not noticed any at the side of main roads. It transpires that the large and sometimes rather elegant establishments which I took to be discotheques, and outside of which I have spotted many a luxury car, are in fact places of prostitution!

Noting my consternation, Paco explained that they were technically hotels; hotels in which many young women from all over the world lived. Of an afternoon or evening they were apt to wander down to the bar for refreshments and quite often struck up a conversation with one of the many male visitors who had popped in for a drink. Sometimes, but not always, they would hit it off so well that they would retire to the girl's room for a short time and whatever took place therein was their own business and technically nothing to do with the hotel.

Técnicamente, técnicamente! But what, I asked, about the morals of the nation? What about the poor, unsuspecting wives at home? Paco shrugged and said, "cada uno a lo suyo" (each to their own), but that he had not set foot in one for a very long time and that, besides, they were, he had been told, getting more and more expensive - the drinks, he said he meant. Perceiving that he was keen to drop the subject, I determined to take it up again with the more candid Alfredo on our next golf outing and get to the bottom of this moral outrage. Until I have done so, I cannot help but suspect every man I see, including Paco, Alfredo, Andy and Trevor - no, perhaps not Trevor - of participating in this loathsome, degenerate practice.

Domingo, 9 de Noviembre

On Friday morning a large delivery van arrived while Pamela was at the bakery and, after signing for the unwelcome consignment, I spent the next half hour carrying bonsai trees through the house and dumping them on the patio. Not two or three, but *thirty* bonsai trees the obsessive chump has sent us, presumably to correctly commemorate each year of our marriage. Even Pamela thought he had overdone it and took the ugliest one next door for Angeles, who immediately gave it to Nora to plant on their plot with the rather sensible intention of trying to make it grow. Following her lead, I took the second most repulsive one to Rocío and Pedro's, where I was offered an untimely can of beer, which I declined, and asked about the scrap metal dealer I had mentioned at the birthday party.

I decided to accept the proffered beverage after all and, while deciding on my line of attack, pointed out that the bonsai was a very low-maintenance 'arbolico' (treelet) which would look very well in the corner of a small to medium-sized patio and that I could easily supply three more for the other corners. At this point Rocío surprised me by saying, "Ernestito, te conozco como si te hubiera parido" (Little Ernesto, I know you as if I had given birth to you), before going on to say that she knew that I had some little transaction in mind and would I be so kind as to tell her what it was all about. Pedro seconded this from within his cloud of smoke, so I decided to lay my cards on the table, so to speak, and share my vision of a beautiful paved patio stretching no more than ten metres from their house and surrounded by a lovely high wooden fence. I would, I said, arrange for the removal of the old cars and other scrap, pay for the patio and fence of their choice, and in return the rest of the land would be legally transferred to my name. Rocío nodded, Pedro puffed and nodded, I nodded, and Rocío said, "No".

"No?" I asked. "No," she repeated, adding that I had obviously never done business with a gypsy before and that, while a 'payo' (non-gypsy) might be seduced by the idea of a pretty little patio, with them it came down to one thing and one thing alone; dinero. She then ushered me out to the scrapyard and paced away from the house, around a pram, and over a broken ladder, before scraping a line in the earth with her slippered foot. From that line onwards, she said, the land *may* be for sale and that it was for me to decide how much I wished to pay for it and for her to accept or decline. To encourage me to offer a good price, she said, she would have the scrap removed very soon.

It was a chastised but hopeful 'Ernestito' who returned home to drink a cup a tea in his bonsai forest and tell Pamela the news of his offer, rebuke, and Rocío's more hard-nosed suggestion. Further chastised for not having consulted her regarding the future disposal of, I quote, 'my mother's money', I took Sancho for a walk and on our return witnessed a flatbed lorry on the bottom track, reversing through our neighbours' flimsy fence, before beginning to extract the first of the rusty cars. The swarthy driver and his mate soon left in a cloud of dust and by the end of the afternoon only a few old plant pots remained on the land which may, nay will, soon be mine. Judging by Rocío's rapid deployment of her workforce, I concluded that if we had had a few Spanish gypsies at the helm of the British motor industry in the 1970s, we might still be making motor cars now.

As I have no intention of turning this journal into a series of golf scorecards, it will suffice to say that Alfredo beat me again yesterday, but by only five shots, before we settled down in the clubhouse to our customary cold beer, mixed nuts, and conversation; a conversation, it must be said, that has left me with a considerably lower opinion of Spanish and certain other men.

After he had accepted my generous gift of four bonsai trees, I broached the subject of the roadside 'clubes' (clubs) which Paco had made me aware of, and nonchalantly asked him his opinion of them. He said that the one on the road to Alicante was by far the best in the area, before asking me if I had a peanut stuck in my throat. I replied that I hadn't and that my reaction was due to the shock of hearing that yet another of my friends - my *married* friends - saw no wrong in frequenting such temples of iniquity. After indulging in a short but hearty spell of laughter, he said that he often went to the 'puticlub' to entertain clients and that most people just went for a drink and a little banter with the girls, as to 'subir' (go upstairs) was very expensive and, for a married man like himself, not quite 'correcto', although it was considered quite acceptable for older single men to indulge from time to time.

Noting my disapproval, he then switched to English - as is his wont when making a point - and said, "But what you want Ernesto? Is better the girls you see on road outside cities and get in car for ten euros? Puticlub very safe and girls can make lot of money if they not put it all up nose," meaning, he then explained, that it was not unusual for the girls to keep their spirits up by indulging in a spot of cocaine snorting. "This is Spain, Ernesto," he went on, "and I think you a little green." "*I* am certainly not a green man!" I protested vehemently, before he assured me that he meant the other kind of green.

Not wishing to appear overly guileless, and remembering the sordid kerb crawling that went on in my old country, I conceded that to go to one of those clubs for a drink was not in itself a sin, but that in England we had a slightly different set of values. "In England, maybe," he said, "but your Scotland friend he there last Wednesday with two old Villeda agricultores. He just have drink, I think, but fat farmer he up stairs like hot bull."

I doubt very much that I shall subject the future reader to these investigative segments of my journal, both out of consideration for their sensibilities and also due to their potentially libellous content. If I do, however, I will make it very clear that when, on the journey home, Alfredo swung gleefully into the 'puticlub' car park, I pointed him very decidedly back onto the road. Laura, Marjorie, and even Ana may turn a blind eye to their husbands' little walks on the wild side, but I strongly suspect that Pamela would not.

With no more festivities on the horizon and Gerald and Lena unlikely to return until next month, this morning I suggested to Pamela that it would be an excellent time for us to take our second road trip. To my surprise she agreed immediately, but to my disappointment then added, "What's it to be then, Madrid or Barcelona? You can check out the trains and hotels and I'll have a look at what's going on in each city," which was not at all what I had in mind, despite my rash promise after the Cuenca trip. Having already decided where I wished to go, I pointed out that at this time of year it would be far more sensible to head south, before praising the historical beauty of Granada and the fascinating and no less historical cultural incongruity of Gibraltar on the warm southern coast.

"That's funny," she said, "because only yesterday at Line Dancing Trevor said he was dying to visit the Alhambra again. Perhaps they'd like to come too, although I can't really see why you'd want to go to see a lump of rock that your country stole from Spain." "Won fair and square," I protested, before remembering my new loyalties and current priorities. After a lengthy debate, Pamela eventually conceded that it did make sense to head south, but that she would *not* travel by road in 'that monstrous cattle truck', meaning my car, and that, if train travel was as impractical as I claimed it to be for my preferred itinerary, the only option was to rope Trevor and Janice in and go in their sensible car.

As Trevor is the only one of my friends still untainted by the recent scandalous revelations, and as Pamela is adamant that she will not repeat the 'horrifying ordeal' of our previous driving tour, I saw no option but to offer that cuddly, cultured couple the opportunity of accompanying us in their car. Without more ado, I called Sancho, took the short stick which he had been coveting ever since I had placed it on the mantelpiece the previous evening, and headed out to see them. The advantage of Sancho's obsession is that I am now able to dispense with his lead, as he would not dream of leaving my side for an instant, lest I hide, lose, or eat his treasure, while the disadvantage is that if I do not throw it at least once a minute, his agitation is such that one cannot relax or walk in a straight line. After about forty throws - alternating arms to maintain muscular symmetry - we reached the gates of Casa Harrison and were greeted first by their vicious, slavering, entirely harmless Alsatian, and shortly afterwards by the jaunty, ever more sprightly, but still stout Trevor.

After insisting yet again that I could not possibly fit Line Dancing into my hectic schedule and hearing all about the vivacious new addition to their troupe - a few weeks of Francisco will produce more pertinent adjectives, I am sure - I told him of our intention to visit Granada and Gibraltar in the very near future and asked him if he and Janice would like to accompany us. "Ah, Granada," he said whimsically, "the Alhambra, the Albayzín, Sacromonte; wonderful! But why Gibraltar?" "The views from the rock," I replied, "the Great Siege Tunnels, St Michael's Cave, the World War Two Tunnels, the Botanic Gardens, the Trafalgar Cemetery, and," running out of memorised attractions, "the apes."

Trevor, still unconvinced, then tried to sell me a far inferior tour, taking in only Granada and a pair of insignificant seaside towns, but I fought doggedly to keep Gibraltar in the itinerary, despite Janice adding weight - in this case only figuratively speaking - to his argument by saying that it was such a trek to get there. "A mere 376 miles," I said, "just six hours in my old but fairly reliable car, and its lack of air conditioning shouldn't be a problem at this time of year, although it is quite warm today."

The perceptive future reader may have noted my subtle insinuation regarding the shortcomings of my vehicle, but Janice saying, "Oh, we'll go in ours; it's ever so economical," rolled so readily off her tongue that I began to smell a fish; an expedient fish, it must be said, but a fish all the same. Our mode of transport secured, I then found myself fighting a doubled-pronged preference for a circular 'Granada plus seaside towns' tour, and it was only when they both admitted to never having visited Gibraltar that I shamed the historian in Trevor into siding with me against a strangely worried-looking Janice, who nonetheless insisted doggedly that the seaside towns could not be dispensed with. Returning to the figurative fish, its smell only grew in intensity when I asked them when they would like us to set off. Their vague responses to this very simple question suggested that an absent but omnipresent influence - and I don't mean God - was exerting strange powers over them. We said our goodbyes, I collected my dog and his appendage, and I headed home to see if I could locate the source of their inspiration.

I found Pamela toying with her herbs, which have flourished despite her flagrant lack of husbandry, and told her that we were to go in Trevor and Janice's nice car and would visit Granada and probably Roquetas de Mar and Mojacár, "and," I added, after observing the gleam of triumph in her eyes, "Gibraltar."

"Oh," she said, half blinded by the gleam in *my* eyes, "Are you sure they want to go there?"

"Oh yes. Your telephone call got you the seaside, but my persuasive powers got me The Rock," and, after indulging in a short bout of mildly demonic laughter, I left her, trowel in hand, and went to put the kettle on.

Pamela had the last laugh once again, however, as when I took her a cup of tea and asked her why, despite her briefing, they had been so vague about the dates of departure, she said, "Because we are setting off on the day when the men come to install the central heating and I still don't know exactly when that will be."

I turned sharply to avoid the gleam and headed inside again, figures whirring in my head, but at least I shall see Granada and Gibraltar before I am left destitute by the central heating installation bill.

Tonight my sane students took Francisco's swaggering entrance in full Line Dancing attire in their stride and, after we had admired his pointy boots with their silly studded leather straps and his tasselled waistcoat which I doubt even Gerald would wear, I asked him if the other participants wore similarly authentic gear. "Ernie wear nice boots," he said, "but lot of ladies wear, how you say, zapatillas de deporte?" "Training shoes, sports shoes, sneakers, or pumps," answered Lola before I could open my mouth. "Yes they dance in sneakies," he went on, "not auténtico like I, but they dance good." "That's interesting," I interrupted, "but how do you say chub in Spanish?"

Receiving only a sigh, a shrug, and a tilt of his cowboy hat, I picked up my freshwater fish cards and found that all but Lola had only remembered perch and carp, which, being percha and carpa in Spanish, hardly counted. By twenty past seven I had drummed dace, barbel, bream, rudd, tench and roach into them successfully, only to be met with one of their periodic rebellious episodes. After insisting that they rebel in English, Alfredo led the mutiny with, "Ernesto, I not know what these fish look like in Spanish or any other lengua. Why we learn?" which was seconded by nods and grunts of agreement from the others. "Line Dancing words better," said Francisco. "Fan kick, heel split, knee pops-" "Yes, yes," I interrupted, "but we learn such useful things as freshwater fish in case we travel to England and fall into conversation with fishermen on the riverbank. Now we will speak about travel. Who has been to Granada?"

This invitation to speak was received with enthusiasm, but as they all tried to speak at once - very much the Spanish way - I was forced to insist upon silence, followed by an orderly raising of hands. It transpired that only Lola and Alfredo had visited Granada - Alfredo on business, which does not count - and that they were, on the whole, a very poorly travelled bunch indeed, with Madrid and Barcelona being the only cities which they had felt they ought to visit at least once. Francisco said he had stayed at three sanatoriums, but had no idea where they were, which was unsurprising under the circumstances. Soon tiring of their mistreatment of my language, I told them about my projected road trip and, as expected, was met with jovial cries of 'Gibraltar, Español!' Mastering my illogical, perhaps hereditary, annoyance at this futile assertion, I counterattacked with the question that Trevor said he had always found very effective; "But what about Ceuta and Melilla, eh?" to which Alfredo replied, "Bah, that just two little bits Africa; without importance. Gibraltar fine big rock and very estratégico. Will be Spanish soon." Remembering that I too will soon be practically Spanish, I resisted the impulse to teach them 'over my dead body' and instead spent the last few minutes attempting to elicit the correct pronunciation of Gibraltar, which only Lola consented to say, before receiving the ironic catcalls of the rest of the class.

After apologising for the fact that we may have to miss a class due to my road trip - news which they took surprisingly well - I bade them goodnight, before settling down with Paco to our almond liqueur and the soothing melodies of Charley Pride. I told him about my land negotiations with my neighbours and asked him how much money I should offer them for the greater part of their plot. His suggestion of €1000 was a pleasant surprise and I said that I had thought it would cost much more, to which he replied that it would, but as Rocío would already have decided on the price, it mattered little what my starting bid was and that I should increase it little by little and with much protestation to prove that I wasn't a soft touch. She probably had in mind, he said, a figure of one million pesetas, but on my asking if gypsies still used the old currency, he laughed and said that nobody did, but that most people still thought in terms of pesetas where larger sums were involved.

One million sounds an awful lot of money in any currency, but then so does six thousand; its equivalent in euros. I comfort myself with the thought that land rarely loses its value, unlike expensive central heating systems.

For the last two days I have employed every spare moment in researching all aspects of our road trip, except the route, which Pamela has printed out from the internet and from which we are not to stray. It is an unadventurous route - straight to Gibraltar on the motorway and straight back to Granada on the same - but I will enlist Trevor's assistance in insisting that we wend our way from Granada to the coast through the reputedly beautiful Alpujarras, unknown to the outside world until an Englishman wrote a book about lemons some years ago. Nerys says it is a wonderful book, which is why I have yet to read it, but I may do so after I have researched and visited the area. After my extensive and continuing research, Trevor may be surprised to find that he is not the only historian in our little party.

My choice of hotels has been approved, but I cannot book them until the central heating people tell us when they are to begin. As Pamela had threatened, it is to be a Spanish company and I very much doubt that the five or six days we are to be away will be sufficient time for them to complete the job. I will not be at all surprised if we return to find them seated atop the still boxed radiators, smoking or chewing bits of straw.

Pamela insists that Nora will be perfectly capable of feeding the poultry and Ernestina, while Sancho will have the run of Andy's finca and is to sleep on their porch, as Ana, like many Spanish people, thinks that dogs are mere animals and should not enter the house. This will be a character-building experience for Sancho and I hope that the fact that he will probably be ignored will cure him of his stick fetish. All that remains, then, is to await the start date, which I trust will be sometime before Christmas.

Domingo, 16 de Noviembre

To my lingering amazement, the house is now packed with boxed radiators, a boiler, lengths of piping, and sundry other items, for work is to commence tomorrow morning! The two men who arrived yesterday afternoon in their smart van looked very efficient and trustworthy and made no attempt to smoke, so my misgivings about letting strangers loose in the house have diminished somewhat. I still very much doubt that they will finish the job in a week, but Pamela has told them very clearly that they must, so they just might. I know I would.

After their departure I threw myself into a frenzy of hotel booking, further historical research, and copious printing of information which has taken up most of my time since then. This afternoon I took Sancho - along with his bed, blanket, lead, bowls and food - to Andy's and hope that he enjoys the new sights, sounds, smells and sticks of his temporary home. Ernestina will have Nora and the heating installers for company, so she can practise her malevolent stare on them for a change. I have given Nora a key on a loop of string and strict instructions regarding the amount of bird and goat feed he is to dispense. I have also invited him to consume some of the eggs in our absence and to prune the fruit trees if he feels like it, to which he mimed his assent. I shall buy them a souvenir of Granada in thanks for their assistance, as I doubt that they have travelled further than a day's cart ride from the village in their lives.

As this road trip will be far more newsworthy than our short excursion last winter, I shall take a notebook in order to write up each day's events while they remain fresh in my memory, although I have done so much research that I almost feel that I have taken the trip already. Pamela says that following the internet street maps around Granada and Gibraltar - and most of our route - will have spoilt the surprise, but I disagree as one cannot hear or smell photographic images.

Lunes, 17 de Noviembre
La Puebla de Don Arsenio - Gibraltar

While Pamela relaxes in a hot bath, I shall write up my account of our fatiguing first day, which sees us installed in a comfortable hotel in the centre of town which, although Pamela says it is rather shabby, meets our humble requirements. Trevor and Janice picked us up at nine this morning, just after the four workmen had arrived with their tools. After telling them where I would like the boiler and the gas deposit - for it is to be propane gas central heating for us - and giving the oldest man front and back door keys on a loop of string, I said goodbye to Ernestina and we 'hit the road'.

As it is a not inconsiderable distance to Gibraltar, Trevor suggested that we share the driving and after he had driven us down the motorway past Lorca - evoking memories of that gory afternoon - I took the wheel on the quiet dual carriageway to Granada and enjoyed the smooth handling of their German saloon car so much that I sped past Granada, ignoring Pamela's comment that it was a pity to go any further, and reached the town of Loja before Trevor and Janice's hunger pains forced me to pull off the motorway and seek a roadside restaurant. Fortified by a wholesome menu del día, Janice then levered herself into the driver's seat, ignored my alternative route suggestion to avoid the toll road, and drove us quite competently past Málaga - where Pamela said it was a pity to go any further - and onto the far busier motorway along the tourism-blighted coast.

After turning off the main motorway and paying our final toll of the day, the rock of Gibraltar came into view, stirring up strange patriotic feelings inside me that I kept to myself, and, after getting lost in the labyrinth of streets that comprises the ugly, bustling town of La Linea, we came out at the other end and crossed the border onto Winston Churchill Avenue, no less. I had expected it to feel quite different in, or on, Gibraltar, but, apart from the street names and the registration plates, it seemed rather like being in Spain, which I might have known as I had already explored it thoroughly on the street map. Said familiarity, however, did enable us to find the hotel straight away and snap up one of their parking spaces. Now we are to go out to dinner I know not where, as, despite my encyclopaedic knowledge of the place, Pamela says I am not to predestine every single event of the trip.

Later: My influence already appears to be on the wane as, after taking us puffing and panting - them, not me - up the hill to a *Moroccan* restaurant, where it must be said the food was delicious and preferable to the English fare which I thought we would have to eat, Trevor then guided us to a pub, insisted that I try the bitter, and coolly announced that tomorrow we are to be picked up from the hotel at half past ten to be taken on a *guided tour* of the place. Before I could protest, Pamela silenced me by laying her hand on my arm and tickling me with her nails, while Janice explained that to get taxis everywhere would be almost as expensive and we would miss out on the knowledgeable guidance of the expert guides. I nodded my acquiescence, Pamela withdrew her hand, and, by way of silent protest, I left the poorly travelled English beer and ordered a small malt whisky.

Once back in our room, I put all my notes back in their folder while Pamela chirruped away, saying that Gibraltar didn't seem so bad after all and that she would find the recipe for the lamb tagine which I had enjoyed so much. I strongly suspect that she has teamed up with Janice and Trevor to shift the balance of power away from me, despite her witnessing my hours of self-sacrificial slaving over the computer.

Martes, 18 de Noviembre
Gibraltar

Having decided to set myself up for the day with the rare treat of a full English breakfast, I was disappointed to be given only a floppy croissant, toast and orange juice, which I had not expected on British territory, but which the others found quite adequate. I had expected Trevor and Janice to require more food to fuel their oversized bodies, but they appear to eat no more than a standard person. Janice says that the Line Dancing is helping them to lose weight, but I am yet to see any perceptible shrinkage and being ferried around the place in a tour bus instead of taking the walking route which I had planned will do little to advance their slimming ambitions.

A shiny 'people carrier' rather than a tour bus pulled up at half past ten sharp and our guide - a suspiciously Spanish-looking young man - greeted us cheerfully and told us that we were to have the car to ourselves, which was some consolation. As we drove up the road towards the rock, I was most relieved to have left my walking plans unsaid, as the length and steepness of the ascent in today's warm weather would have caused instant mutiny. If truth be told, taking the guided tour did have its advantages and my studies enabled me to confirm the veracity of our helpful guide's information about St Michael's Cave, the Great Siege Tunnels, the Moorish castle and all the other sites which we visited along with rather too many other people. The views across the straits to Africa were most impressive and the apes most amusing, especially the one Pamela photographed eating prawn cocktail flavoured crisps given to it by an ignorant tourist, before she snapped another one peering over a wall in much the same way that Nora looks over my fence. We then descended the hill and were driven along the coastal road past the impressive mosque and less impressive Catholic shrine - both testimony to the tolerance of British rule - and were finally deposited back at the marina where we drank a cool beer in the sun with the other tourists.

That, indeed, is quite enough tourist talk, as the purpose of this journal is to charter the course of my integration into Spanish life and not an account of what any Tom, Dick or expat can pay someone to show them. Returning to the subject of this journal - namely, me and my experiences - what then are my impressions of Gibraltar? Should it be British, Spanish, or Gibraltareño? Rather tired now after tonight's Italian meal washed down by several glasses of red wine, I can think of nothing better to say than that its uniqueness is quite unique and should perhaps not be tampered with until everyone agrees that it is time for a change. Pamela says that she has enjoyed the visit and is looking forward to seeing Granada, so in that respect I am in an infinitely stronger position than after the first day of the Cuenca trip.

Miércoles, 19 de Noviembre
Gibraltar - Granada

Yet another sunny November day and after Trevor had driven us straight to Granada in a little under three hours, we checked in to our hotel in the city centre and went out to eat. While in Gibraltar my authority was undermined by the commissioning of a paid guide, I soon saw that Trevor's familiarity with Granada would leave me playing second, or even third, fiddle here too, but at least my lack of responsibility would allow me to relax and enjoy the city. Also, if anything went wrong, it would not be my fault.

In Granada a curious system is in place whereby one is given free food every time one buys a drink. The secret, Trevor told us, is to know the bars where they dispense the most succulent tapas, which he assured us he did. Thus after four glasses of beer in four different establishments, I had almost eaten my fill and was looking forward to one more tapa with my coffee to see me right for the afternoon. This time, however, the food failed to materialise and I was forced to order a cake, but even so, it is a merry and economical way to eat and left me wondering how they actually made any money. Either they are foolish to a man, or in the rest of Spain they are overcharging, so I will suggest to the owners of the two village bars that they institute this practice right away - or perhaps just in the clean bar as even the paid tapas in the dirty bar are of dubious provenance.

After lunch we walked to the Albyzín area and strolled up the charming cobbled streets until we reached a viewpoint called the Mirador de San Nicolas, from where we looked across the valley to see the Alhambra in all its magnificence with the imposing Sierra Nevada in the distance. It is not surprising that the Moors, already expelled from the rest of Spain, hung on for grim death in this city. After they had finally been chucked out, Trevor told us, the Spaniards, after Charles V had built a palace right in the middle of it, allowed the Alhambra to fall into a state of shocking disrepair until in the 19th century travellers from more civilised countries made them realise that it might be worth patching up. Trevor told us many facts and figures, which I ticked off my mental list, before I added that the Duke of Wellington had planted an English elm wood in the park in 1812. This interesting fact was met by polite nods from Trevor and Janice and, I thought, the unusually intimate slipping of Pamela's hand into my left-hand trouser pocket. In a split second I realised that as Pamela was standing on my right and has arms of normal length it could not be her hand, so I grasped the wrist and found a small Moorish-looking boy on the end of it. I was all for calling the police on Pamela's mobile telephone, but Trevor warned me that his larger companions might well arrive before they did, so I contented myself with pointing at the Alhambra and suggesting to the boy that he look to it for inspiration. On releasing him, he rubbed his wrist, called me a 'tonto del culo' (silly arse), and ran off down the street, so I fear that my well-intentioned advice will go unheeded.

On our stroll back to the hotel we popped into the

magnificent cathedral which Trevor told us, and I already knew, was built after demolishing the mosque - the usual practice in the recently re-Christianised Spain of the day. Thank goodness, he said, that they had not destroyed the incredible mosque of Córdoba and had contented themselves with their other annoying habit of plonking a church in the middle of it. When Pamela and I visit Seville and Córdoba - a trip I have projected for late 2009 or early 2010 - I will ensure that this larger than life font of all knowledge does not accompany us. Both Trevor and Janice, it must be said, are good travelling companions in all respects except for Trevor's excessive didactic ramblings.

After a short rest at the hotel we chose to 'tapear' (eat tapas) once again in the evening, which was both pleasant and economical, but in the long run would turn one into a dipsomaniac or soft drinks addict. Tomorrow we visit the Alhambra with the tickets that I thoughtfully booked in advance, so I will now read through my notes in the hope of remembering some snippets of information which Trevor may neglect to tell us.

Jueves, 20 de Noviembre
Granada - La Alhambra - Granada

This sunny morning at nine o'clock we collected our tickets at the entrance to the Alhambra and entered along with a multitude of multinational visitors, most of whom looked quite cultured, like ourselves, and a few who would have been just as happy at Disneyland. Conscious of our strict half hour time slot in which to visit the Nasrid Palaces, Trevor led us first to the Alcazabar (fortress or citadel) which he told us was the oldest part of the Alhambra where building had commenced in the ninth century and was finished sometime in the thirteenth. "Yes," I said, wishing to add colour to these dull facts, "and Mohammed the First built the walls and the three towers," which aroused the interest of an ancient, emaciated American lady who asked me in which century he had done that. "Oh, in about the eleventh," I guessed, much to the amusement of Trevor, who positioned himself behind the lady and held up thirteen fingers - not all at once, of course - with a big grin on his fat face.

After this minor humiliation, I decided to dispense with my other post-it notes and just enjoy the rest of our visit, which, on reflection, was by far the best thing I could have done. After enjoying the splendid views from the watchtower, we moved on to the palace which, impressive though it is, Charles V could just as easily have built somewhere else, before wandering about in the more rundown Upper Alhambra until it was our turn to enter the Nasrid Palaces.

Words cannot describe the beauty of these building and their exquisite artwork, so I shall not attempt to do so, but I strongly urge the future reader to pay a visit and see for him or herself. I doubt that the published journal will contain photographs, but if it does, the one of me looking pensively at the fountain in the Patio de los Leones will be sure to feature, so long as the gaggle of Japs to my left can be eliminated from the digital image. After resting awhile in the Garden of the Partal, we made our way down to the Generalife, where the Arab kings relaxed to the playing of the fountains on the warm summer evenings. I found the patios and gardens truly inspiring and reflected that when I have secured most of Rocío and Pedro's plot and the whole of Angeles and Nora's, there *may* be land to spare on which to create a decorative feature - on a much more modest scale, of course - on which to feast my weary eyes after a long day's toil on the productive section of my huge plot.

The morning had flown by and it was soon time to vacate the premises to allow the afternoon shift to enter. My thoughts of Nora's land had reminded me that I intended to buy them a souvenir of our visit so, with this in mind, I asked the taxi driver - for the two slimmers in our party had insisted that it was too far to walk - to take us to some souvenir shops. He dropped us off near Alcaicería Street, which proved to be an alleyway full of Arabic and other souvenir shops, where we browsed until I came across the perfect gift. As Nora smokes his pipe incessantly, I decided to buy him a large cachimba, or water pipe, which, if he takes to it, will oblige him to smoke in a stationary position rather than through other people's houses. Pamela reminded me that Angeles does not smoke, but I pointed out that the pipe was so decorative that it would double up as an ornament. Unconvinced, she bought her a souvenir plate with pictures of the Alhambra, so I think they will consider themselves well rewarded for the trifling chores which I trust they are carrying out.

Later on, during our *Chinese* evening meal, which turned out to be excellent, Trevor and I persuaded the girls that our route to Roquetas de Mar tomorrow simply must take in the wonderful white villages of the Alpujarras and that, despite the odd twist and turn, we would have to spend no more than three hours in the car. Pamela said that she hoped it would be more interesting than the wastelands of inland Valencia that I had dragged her round earlier in the year and that at least this time we would be in a proper car.

The sun was rising above the Sierra Nevada when we took the road south from Granada this morning. Before cresting the rise on the dual carriageway, after which point the tourists would head down to the coast and explorers like ourselves east to the Alpujarras, Trevor let out an almighty sigh which made me fear that his overburdened body had finally succumbed to a heart attack, but which was, he explained, his replica of King Boabdil's famous last sigh when he had turned to see Granada for the last time after being booted out in 1492. What was really fascinating, he said, was that on that fateful 2nd January Christopher Columbus, who was to inadvertently discover America later that same year, was in the city and actually witnessed poor old Boabdil kissing the hands of King Ferdinand and Queen Isabella before they ushered him through the gate. After that, he said, while I suppressed a sigh of my own, they gave Columbus the cash for his famous first voyage and, with most of the Moors taken care of, set about expelling the Jews, unless they agreed to become papists, which they weren't terribly keen on doing. "Look," I said, "there's the turn off to the Alpujarras," before unfolding my map and naming some of the places we were to pass through in the hope of ending Trevor's fourth form history class. "The Moors held out down here for another eighty years," he went on, "until they finally shooed them out and just left a few to show the ignorant Christians how to use their superb irrigation system."

By this time we had driven through the spa town of Lanjarón and were heading towards Órgiva, where Janice said that the fellow who wrote the lemons book lived. "Bah," said Trevor, unstoppable today, "popular stuff and not at all historical. Gerald Brenan was your man when it came to writing about the Alpujarras; about Spain in general, in fact. We can see the house where he lived in the 1920s later on today." "Let's stop for a twenty-first century coffee, shall we?" said Pamela, which I thought both witty and supportive, as she knows how much I hate being told things that I do not already know.

Órgiva is the largest town in the Alpujarras and contains a mixture of normal local folk, a few tourists, and a disturbing number of throwbacks from the hippy age, whenever and wherever that was. These foreign people, some considerably older than myself, loped and lurched around the streets in their unseemly attire and, had Gerald not already embarked upon his new industrious life, I would have had to bring him here to show him how he would end up if he continued to spurn the norms of polite society. A man in his sixties dressed in pyjamas with a shiny purple head atop the grizzled remains of a once flourishing ponytail is not a pretty sight, but one can only pity these people who must have reached a point of social marginalisation and ostracism from which they have found there is no return. Pamela disagreed with my, and I quote, 'narrow-minded bigotry' and said that they were a jolly sight better off here than being stuck in an English suburb, mowing their lawns and having grandchildren foisted upon them every weekend and school holiday.

Not all these 'hippies' were of retirement age, however, and I wondered aloud how they kept body and soul together. Janice, who is quiet but observant, said that by the look of the calloused hands of two young men who had just passed, they might well be engaged in agricultural pursuits. "Yes," said

Pamela, "they probably really do live the way you say you want to live, but never will," to which I replied smartly that it was not I who had insisted on expensive, unnecessary and - plucking a word from the old Gerald's vocabulary - *bourgeois* central heating. This little tiff rather soured our coffee - figuratively speaking, for the coffee was excellent - until Trevor's commentary regarding Brenan's book, 'South from Granada' bored us all into serenity once more.

Yegen, where Brenan had lived, was in fact to be our next port of call and shortly after commencing the 'forty-odd ever so picturesque miles', as Trevor called them, I was ever so pleased and relieved that it was not I who had chosen the route. Picturesque though it undoubtedly was, especially the view up the valley from Pampaneira to Capileira - villages named by the Galician people who were imported into the area to replace the Moors - to say that the road was 'a mite twisty', was like calling Mount Everest a bit of a slog. There weren't just bends, there were bends within bends, and at times one could have sworn that we had driven full circle before the next curve took us round again the other way. Pamela, who is rather prone to car sickness, did not appreciate this spiralling stairway to heaven and declined very firmly Trevor's suggestion that we 'just nip up to Capileira to take a peek'. In the pretty village of Pitres she instructed him to stop, got out of the car, and requested me to squeeze my long legs into the back seat. On protesting, she asked me if I would prefer her to decorate my head with projectile vomit, which I did not, so we swapped places and went on our way towards the village of Trevélez. On perusing the map, I saw that the road climbed six miles to the village, before descending six miles down the other side of the valley to a point not a mile from where we had started from. I concluded that the resourceful Moors had not got round to building a short cut for the less gifted Christians to use, but I did not share this with Pamela, who by this time had her head out of the window as Sancho is wont to do, albeit with less ear flapping. On reaching Trevélez, there was no doubt in Pamela's mind that we were going to modify our plans and take lengthy break, so Trevor obediently parked the car and, after finding our land legs, we headed up the hill into the village.

Trevélez, Trevor informed us, is higher up than Ben Nevis and is in fact the highest village in Spain, if you don't count an insignificant ski resort somewhere or other. It is certainly beautiful and remote, nestling as it does on the side of the towering mountain, but I am sure that the top of Ben Nevis does not suffer from the same overabundance of handicraft shops, tourist accommodation and coach parties which this village's famous cured ham industry has spawned. Up here the cold, dry weather is perfect for curing the hams and, as a consequence, people travel from miles around to buy pottery, fans, wineskins, and calendars with Trevélez written on them. Of the two coach parties trudging around the place and who, by the look of them, were up from taking the waters at Lanjarón, I did not see a single person carrying a leg of ham; indeed many looked too frail to carry a ham sandwich. That the loathsome blight of tourism has reached such an isolated spot makes me fear even for the future serenity of La Puebla de Don Arsenio and it may well be in my best interests to publish these journals under a pseudonym, lest I cause a similar influx of undesirable elements to that produced by the lemons book in Órgiva.

No such influx was caused, Trevor said as he drove us

slowly down the valley, by the former residence of the esteemed writer Gerald Brenan in the village of Yegen and, when we finally arrived, I saw that this was indeed the case. After strolling round the deserted village and admiring the commemorative wall tiles on the house where he had lived, we adjourned to a scruffy bar for refreshments, where Trevor asked the lady owner if Brenan's memory was still alive in the village. She knew, she said, that he had knocked up his maid, but apart from that it was not until fifty years later that the mayor put the plaque up in the hope of attracting tourists. When she had shuffled off into the kitchen, a rather disappointed Trevor said that there was no reference to his canoodling with the home help in the book and that, in any case, it was probably too well written to ever appeal to the masses, which is sufficient reason for me to borrow it as soon as we get home.

After driving through the picturesque town of Ugíjar without being obliged to make yet another pit stop, we soon reached a better road which took us over the final range of hills and down towards the large town of El Ejido near the coast. Although our descent afforded us a fine view of the sea, the fact that the town is surrounded by miles of plastic sheeting means that the only 'tourists' are the many hued foreign workers who sweat and toil in those makeshift greenhouses in order that the rest of Europe can eat a vast array of fruit and vegetables all year round. These were Janice's words, not mine, but as a traditional horticulturalist who firmly believes in consuming each fruit of the soil in due season, I sympathise with the lot of these poor immigrants and shall only use the small greenhouse which I intend to place strategically in front of the ugly gas deposit for seedlings. That or the shed - for obscuring the gas deposit, not for seedlings. (Revise or remove stupid sentence.)

After circumnavigating El Ejido, we popped onto the dual carriageway and in no time at all had emerged from the plastic sheets and entered the resort town of Roquetas de Mar. The drive down from Granada had taken us eight hours or, as Pamela said from her prostrate position in the front seat, "just five hours more than if we had taken the proper road." Pamela's suffering aside, I would not have missed the Alpujarras for the world and firmly intend to return and spend more time there, but I fear that unless they install helipads - which the tourist board is no doubt considering - I shall have to find another travelling companion.

After the splendour of Granada and the beauty of the Alpujarras, Roquetas de Mar is something of an anti-climax, but Pamela says that the sea, the sand, and the excellent weather forecast make it the perfect location in which to spend a relaxing, carefree and car-free day, so it looks like that is what we shall be doing.

Sábado, 22 de Noviembre
Roquetas de Mar, Almería

After my mammoth journal entries of the last few days, today there is relatively little to report. After leaving our nondescript hotel shortly after ten, we sauntered along the pleasant seafront to see the castle and the lighthouse, before ambling back to take the first of our many refreshment breaks. Roquetas used to be a fishing village and it must be said that it has not been ruined as much as most other resorts, but there is little for a practical man such as myself to do here. Pamela, on the other hand, found it attractive and said that it would be a pleasant place to spend the winter, which after this week's cripplingly expensive central heating installation, I found rather disconcerting and said so. "Oh," she replied, "I don't mean now, I mean when we are old, or when I am old and you are pushing up the daisies," and, on seeing my shocked expression, "There is great longevity in my family, you know."

I told her in no uncertain terms that with my healthy, hard-working lifestyle I would probably live to be a hundred and would have to lose most of my faculties in order to find a tourist resort an acceptable place of residence. Remembering the presence of Trevor and Janice, who will almost certainly not live to a great age due to the great bulk which their hearts have to propel round each day, I skilfully changed the subject by asking Trevor about tomorrow's route. He told us that it was only a short, straight drive to Mojácar and could be made more interesting by making a short detour into the Cabo de Gata Natural Park, whose protected villages and coastline would appeal to me. Seeing Pamela's eyes narrowing, he quickly produced a map and pointed out the relative straightness of the roads and the shortness of the detour, which convinced her that another day of torture was not being devised. On the subject of longevity, the huge paella which we ate at midday followed by a substantial dinner in a *Dutch* restaurant, where the food was excellent, will do little to extend our lives and it will be with some relief that I return to my frugal peasant's diet and brisk walks with Sancho the day after tomorrow.

Domingo, 23 de Noviembre
Roquetas de Mar - Mojácar

On the first cloudy day of our trip we were on the road by
ten and as we bowled along the motorway which cut through
the arid landscape, I spotted Almería on our right and asked
Trevor if there was anything of interest to see there. "Oh, not
much," he said, "apart from the tenth century fortress
overlooking the city, but it's a bit over-restored for my liking
and after the Alhambra it's nothing to write home about."

Denied this architectural experience due to lack of research, I
saw little else of interest in this dry countryside and it was not
until we neared the coast that I began to appreciate the stark
beauty of this barren wilderness. On driving into La Isleta del
Moro, I felt that I had at last found a Spanish seaside village to
my liking, with only a few new buildings on the outskirts and a
quaint little jetty which afforded splendid views of the sea and
the hills to the south. Being Sunday, however, many other,
mostly Spanish, people had also descended on this isolated
spot, so, after a stroll and a coffee, we headed off up the coast
to Las Negras, where the square white houses have been
replicated somewhat more liberally, but which still conserves
its charm. After a stroll on the pebbly beach, we ate a light
lunch of fish and salad before heading inland to take the
motorway to Mojácar and thus, Trevor said, avoid the ugly
cement works at Carbonaras and the huge, illegally built hotel
at Algarrobico which even the Spanish authorities will surely
be shamed into demolishing someday.

After the delightful discovery of what must be one of the few
unspoilt stretches left on the Spanish Mediterranean coastline,

Mojácar's beach resort, while much more developed, was also an acceptable place to stay and we soon located our modestly priced hotel which, though Pamela thinks it scruffy, is right next to the beach. As I write I feel very full after the succulent steak I ate at the *Argentinian* restaurant where we dined and it will be a great relief to my stomach and my wallet to return home tomorrow, although I might have mentioned this already.

Lunes, 24 de Noviembre
Mojácar - La Puebla de Don Arsenio

After a brief visit to the pretty village of Mojácar, marred only by the fact that every other house is a souvenir or craft shop, we drove back up the motorway and it was with a mixture of relief and foreboding that we said our goodbyes to our travelling companions and I put my key in the lock of our front door. Expecting to find the house turned upside down amid a chaos of metal tubing, boxes, and - as it was just after two - lunching workmen, imagine my surprise when I found the house in pristine condition and with radiators in every room! This miracle, it turned out, was partly due to Pamela having also contracted *decorators* to come in at the weekend to patch up and paint all the imperfections left by the installation. To my protests that my DIY skills were advanced enough to carry out such simple work and avoid the extra cost, she replied that the extra expense was so trifling compared to the cost of the central heating that it was not worth worrying about.

On the kitchen table they had left some booklets, a sheet of instructions, and an envelope which Pamela scooped up from under my nose and put in her jeans pocket. The bill, she said, was none of my business as it was her 'treat' and would only make me ill anyway. Rather than protesting and being told once again that it was her mother's money, I nodded placidly and made for the back door to see if my animals were still alive, which they were, and to inspect my new gas cylinder. They had installed the large, horizontal cylinder at the bottom of the plot, as instructed, and the fence was miraculously intact. It is white in colour and, despite the gas company's name in unnecessarily large letters, is not as offensive to the eye as I had feared. The pipeline to the house will have cost me a few carrots and cabbages, but its entry through the wall into the kitchen where the boiler has been installed has also been repaired and painted, so there is nothing for me to do but read the instructions, switch it on, and see how well it works.

After checking that the birds and Ernestina had enough feed and noting that the residences of each were spotlessly clean, I was rather glad that we had bought Nora and Angeles nice presents, until I noticed that Nora had divested my fruit trees of most of their branches, leaving them in a most forlorn and stumpy condition, which I sincerely hope is the way that God intended them to be pruned. When I returned to the house the temperature had risen perceptibly as Pamela had followed the workmen's instructions to switch it on and 'darle caña' ('give it some welly'). By the time I returned from Andy's with Sancho, the temperature was at thirty degrees and still rising, so it is safe to say that the system works. I also returned with an invitation to the 'bautizo' of Ana and Andy's baby on Sunday 14th December, after which holy celebration a pig will be slaughtered. Andy insists that he does not intend to 'blood' little Andrés and that carrying out the 'matanza' is merely to kill two birds - a pig and a christening - with one stone. He also assured me that Nora has not slaughtered my fruit trees and said that he would be happy to relieve me of a couple of spare bonsais.

Before settling down to our respective chores, we decided to take our neighbours their presents and pick up the door keys. After being received with a series of whoops and shrieks from Angeles as if we had been away for a year, we thanked them for their help and gave them their gifts. Angeles was delighted with her Alhambra plate and said that it had not changed at all since they had visited it on their honeymoon, while Nora was most perplexed by his cachimba. I explained that it was reputed to be a relaxing way of smoking in one's own home, sitting down, and, after showing him the special tobacco and the little cubes of charcoal, I read out the instructions while he nodded and pulled odd faces. Whether he uses it or not is immaterial to me and as Angeles said that it would look well on the mantelpiece, we might have dispensed with the plate after all.

Having described the events of the day, I must now set down my reflections regarding our road trip. I consider the trip to have been an almost unqualified success and now believe that travelling in company has certain advantages, the chief of which is that when something goes wrong, one can blame it on someone else. Had Pamela and I travelled alone through the Alpujarras at my instigation and in my vehicle, I very much doubt that another car trip would have been permitted for a very long time, if ever. Companions are also an aid to conversation during the long hours of relative idleness and, despite Trevor's sometimes excessive historical monologues, they were, on the whole, pleasant company. What would I change, were I to relive the journey? I would spend more time in the Alpujarras rather than lazing about in seaside resorts and would dispense with the need to eat expensive, though delicious, meals every day. I would take more extensive walks instead of pottering about like old age pensioners and I would eschew taxis and guided tours. Apart from that, I would not change a thing.

I perceive that Pamela has finally switched the central heating off and I trust that it will remain off until the really cold weather starts.

Jueves, 27 de Noviembre

Having rested my weary writing hand for two days, I have several things to report, the first of which is my ongoing dispute with my wife regarding her use, or abuse, of the central heating. On getting up on Tuesday morning, I thought that spring had arrived, such was the warmth of the house, and on inspection I found that the central heating had been set to come on at seven o'clock and to stay on at a temperature of twenty degrees until eleven o'clock in the evening. It appeared that Pamela had overcome her aversion to instruction manuals and, after turning the thermostat down to sixteen, I took Sancho out for a short walk in the bracing morning air. On my return the thermostat had been raised to *twenty-one* degrees, which was in itself enough to make me break out into a sweat.

By way of silent protest I changed into shorts and a summer vest before taking my seat for breakfast and proceeded to mop my brow between each spoonful of cornflakes. "It's lovely and warm, isn't it?" said Pamela as she leafed through a magazine. "Positively tropical, but one's body is supposed to adjust to winter temperatures, and the cost will be astronomical." "Nineteen," she replied. "Seventeen," I countered. "We'll try eighteen degrees, then," she said, "but don't tamper with my thermostat again. I will not suffer from the cold like last winter and it will save you the trouble of lighting that dirty stove."

Since then I have not touched *her* thermostat, but continue to wear short trousers in the house and trust that when the gas deposit empties and we are faced with the considerable cost of refilling it, she will see the error of her ways.

Whether it is because of my week long absence or due to her having had Nora and Angeles for company I do not know, but Ernestina had begun to eye me so resentfully that I decided to take her out to pasture yesterday afternoon. After explained to Pamela that I was going to cool off for a couple of hours, I attached a longish rope to her neck - Ernestina's neck - gave Sancho his stick, put on my straw hat, and headed for the Harrison's track. Ernestina has grown considerably since I dragged her back from Andy's three months ago and she towed me powerfully through the mercifully empty village streets until, on finding her first clump of herbage by the roadside, she began to munch away heartily. Although conscious of the fact that this was her first truly fresh food for a long time and feeling rather guilty that I had not taken her out before, I was nevertheless quite eager to get her off the road and away from the mocking stares of passing motorists. This proved to be more difficult than I anticipated but, after throwing Sancho's stick down the track, I managed to drag her a hundred yards before tying her to a tree and weighing up the situation.

After throwing Sancho's stick for the sixth time, I had one of my brainwaves and fished his lead out of my jacket pocket and clipped it to his collar, which I then loosened slightly. I then collected a small but appetising bunch of weeds and pulled the stalks through his collar, before untying Ernestina and skilfully guiding Sancho in front of her. This rather difficult two-armed manoeuvre enabled us to make some headway as the goat doggedly strove to catch up with the dog and relieve him of his weedy burden. My aim was to reach a clearing a few hundred yards ahead where I would be able to tie Ernestina to a tree with enough rope to graze freely and myself sit down on the low wall like a regular goatherd. I had almost reached my objective when I saw a figure appear up ahead and, fearing that it was the perambulating frequenter of the dirty bar, I panicked, let go of the rope, and yanked the weeds from Sancho's collar.

Imagine my surprise when the approaching walker was in fact Trevor out for an afternoon stroll. Knowing that as a fellow Englishman he would find nothing unusual in my experimental goat propulsion method, I explained the situation before we set about recapturing the goat, who had reached the clearing and appeared to be making a bid for freedom. Trevor, unwilling to try to match the goat for speed, urged patience and suggested that we let her graze for a while. This she did, but when a waft of wind brought the smell of succulent olive trees to her nostrils, she headed off towards them and began tucking into the leaves on the lower branches. This flagrant consumption of private property spurred us into action and, on Trevor suggesting that we employ a pincer movement, we approached her slowly from either side. On our first attempt, Trevor got within a yard of the rope before she bolted back towards the clearing, and on the second I came even closer, but the crack of a twig made her whisk the rope from under my nose. When we had regrouped, Trevor explained that the pincer movement was first used successfully by Hannibal at the Battle of Cannae, but admitted that heavily armoured Romans were probably easier to capture than goats. Not wishing to hear the statistics from the battle, however, and feeling most irate about Ernestina's ungratefulness, I decided to put into practice a more elementary form of attack, namely running straight at her while her back was turned and throwing myself full length at the rope.

When Trevor had stopped clapping and I had dusted myself down, he took the rope while I recovered my glasses, before I tied her so closely to a tree stump that she could eat nothing. After resting for a while, but before Trevor had time to draw parallels with famous military ambushes, we headed back to our respective homes. Ernestina came fairly quietly, but it will be a long time before I take her out again. How *do* goatherds make their beasts follow them around? The internet has thrown up no solutions and I shall have to seek advice from the experts.

My subsequent English class was happily uneventful and, after explained that my severely grazed elbow was due to tripping up on my plot, we made good progress with my new combined tenses flashcards. Francisco endures in his delusion that Line Dancing can take the place of working for a living and, so long as this remains the case, I foresee no traumatic episodes. I told Pamela afterwards that it was so warm in the classroom that I had had to open the window - in November - and that the thermostat is surely rigged to deceive the consumer. As she did not believe me, the next time I go to the ferretería I will buy thermometers and put one in every room.

Domingo, 30 de Noviembre

I awoke to light rain yesterday morning and, after firmly rejecting Alfredo's telephonic appeal to call off our game, made a light breakfast in the sweltering kitchen, before turning the thermostat down by a quarter of a degree and leaving the house with high hopes of a long-awaited victory.

When we arrived and Alfredo had grumpily inserted himself into his new waterproofs, I teed off into a drizzle all too reminiscent of countless past games, but which I sensed was to come to my aid today. Sure enough, after six holes I was three shots clear and, although my legs were slightly damp, this was infinitely preferable to the greenhouse effect that the plastic suit was having on Alfredo, who was sweating more than in midsummer. Pressing home my advantage as we played on in near silence - apart from Alfredo's huffing and the creaking and swishing of his trousers - I was seven shots clear by the tenth and had the taste of victory on the tip of my wet tongue. (Revise: one's tongue is always wet, whatever the weather.)

It was at this point that the rain ceased, Alfredo packed away his fisherman's outfit, and he began to employ all the distractionary tactics that I had taught him before fair play was introduced many months ago. He asked me if I was happy with the central heating installation, which I said I was, before observing that house prices had begun to drop and that one would soon be able to buy a whole finca for an amount that only six months ago would have bought only a small flat. "Good," I said in English, with the intention of evoking my indomitable classroom manner, "that means that I will get my neighbours' land more cheaply," before hitting my careful drive straight down the fourteenth fairway. He lapsed into silence for a while, intent on his game, and managed to pull back three shots, before, realising that he was running out of holes, he began to recount 'puticlub' adventures - of his youth, he said - in a desperate attempt to shock me into losing concentration. A veteran of many a tall, 'blue' golf club tale, I did not flinch and after an ultra-conservative last three holes I emerged victorious by two shots.

Unwilling as I always am to gloat over the failings of others, I ordered our beers and mixed nuts before we took our seats in a quiet corner of the lounge. Alfredo then insisted that his bawdy tales were mostly untrue and had happened a long time ago, but, resisting the impulse to point out the contradictory nature of his statement, I instead turned the subject away from his depravity and onto money matters. On asking him how much I should offer my neighbours for their land, he said that they would take one million, but for me to offer them half a million first. When I said that one million pesetas was the price that Paco had mentioned, he replied that pieces of land of that size always sold for one million, unless the owners were desperate, in which case they sold for half a million. On mentioning his dastardly statements about plummeting house prices, he said that he had not spoken entirely in jest, but that village or country land was a different matter as much pride was at stake, especially among gypsies, who always liked to come out on top when dealing with us 'payos'.

On returning home and still feeling strong after my historic victory, I lost no time in going to call on Rocío and Pedro with the intention of putting my cards on the table, so to speak, but not before jotting down peseta/euro price equivalents on a post-it note which I popped into my shirt pocket. Rocío's greeting was as effusive as Pedro's was nebulous, and after presenting them with another bonsai tree - having forgotten to bring them a present back from our travels - I said that I had come to speak to them about the purchase of their land. "Habla, habla, cariño," (speak, speak, darling) said Rocío, so I made an offer of half a million pesetas. Pedro coughed a cloud of thick smoke, Rocío laughed, and I upped my offer to six hundred thousand. No, she said, I must do better. Seven hundred thousand produced shaking of heads, while eight hundred thousand caused a flurry of tutting. This seemed to me a very one-sided and somewhat humiliating way of doing business and I suggested that it might make things easier if she named her price. She swore that she had no figure in mind, but that she would recognise the right price when she heard it. Tired of this gypsy palaver, I bid them good day and returned home. When I am feeling strong again I shall ask Pamela for her blessing before making my *final* offer of six thousand euros, as I refuse to utter the obsolete word 'pesetas' again.

Viernes, 5 de DICIEMBRE 2008

The price I paid for my famous golfing victory last Saturday was that the wet legs I suffered in my quest for flexibility and coolness produced a nasty cold and cough which has laid me low until today. I shan't be quite fit enough to play again tomorrow and so shall remain the current victor at least until our next duel.

Trevor was kind enough to bring me his copy of the Brenan book 'South from Granada' and I have spent many a pleasant hour reclined upon the sofa reliving the young Englishman's move to the then completely isolated village of Yegen in the 1920s with his two thousand books and the noble intention of educating himself. Mr Brenan, in his way, was even more adventurous than myself and integrated most thoroughly into the little community, as well as walking enormous distances for no apparent reason. His one failing, in my opinion, was his neglecting to buy and tend a plot of fertile Alpujarran land and become as horticulturally self-sufficient as I almost am. Still, nobody is perfect and he did go on to write great books about Spain which I have not yet found the time to do, but then I do not have servants catering to my every whim; including ones not mentioned in the book.

Our warm house has been a cosy place in which to convalesce and I have refrained from protesting about the temperature, preferring instead to concentrate my efforts on securing Pamela's casting vote regarding the purchase of our neighbours' plot. While she still insists that we don't need the land, I have managed to convince her that it is a good investment, so long as I do not exceed the regulation million. To ensure the success of my final bid, I will now bide my time as I did with the purchase of Integración, which I still think was a bargain, despite Alfredo's suspicions that the agent's commission was unusually high. It is true that the substantial cash portion of the payment, which they had insisted on, went into the agent's briefcase, but I assumed that this was for reasons of security. I may ask Alfredo to investigate this matter further, although Pamela has warned me that the truth may lay me up for another week.

Martes, 9 de Diciembre

My still fatigued condition prevented me from celebrating the two national holidays which have just taken place. Having said that, the only perceptible changes to village life were that the bars were fuller on Saturday - el Día de la Constitución Española - and that there was more toing and froing from the church on yesterday's Día de la Inmaculada Concepción, as well as the bars being even fuller than on Saturday.

Speaking of the church, Andy has told me that the demands of the 'matanza' next Sunday will mean that those responsible for it - namely his father-in-law and assorted cronies - will not be able to attend the baptism in church as at that time they will be up to their elbows in pig innards. Keen to be present throughout this rural ritual, I said that I would be by their side to offer my assistance in getting the gory stuff out of the way before the more refined, religious or baby-loving contingent arrived after the service. He regretted that he would have to absent himself to 'film the wetting' as he would love to see my reaction to the 'carnage', where the sights, sounds and smells often had a great impact on first timers such as myself.

Laughing off this absurd suggestion of squeamishness, I insisted that although I might well become a vegetarian at some point in the not too distant future, I was still a meat-eater and should therefore see at first hand how my chops, fillets and sausages were extracted from the animal - in this case one of his smiling pigs. "In that case," he said, "be there at the crack of dawn wearing your oldest clothes. If you have an old red shirt, wear that." Undaunted by his Scottish histrionics, I assured him that I would be there before the sun rose - which the internet later informed me will be at 8.14am - and would be 'dressed to kill', which I thought rather witty. While 'online' I also came across a short video of a 'matanza de cerdo', but refrained from watching it because I do not wish to spoil the surprise as I very nearly did by travelling almost every inch of Gibraltar on the street viewing facility.

Jueves, 11 de Diciembre

Pamela has been poor company since Gerald telephoned yesterday evening to say that he doubted very much whether he and Lena would be able to visit us until early next year. She registered her displeasure by passing the phone straight to me, whereupon my son informed me that the detailed negotiations he was now involved in with his suppliers, along with Frau

Krankl's strong desire to enjoy the company of her daughter and prospective son-in-law over Christmas, made it more expedient to stay there, although if his mother was going to 'get her lederhosen in a twist' he would have to consider coming alone.

I urged him - very quietly - to do no such thing, as his future business prospects had to take priority and that it was also very important to cement his ties with Lena's family. On asking me why this was so important, I reminded him that he was fast approaching thirty and that if the strain on his scalp of so many years of pony tail wearing made his hair fall out, he would be hard pushed to find another mate of Lena's calibre. He thought this a great joke and also solemnly promised to ring on Christmas Day *and* New Year's Day and to visit without fail in January, when he would begin to relieve the 'bourgeois Brits' of their money. Secretly satisfied by the prospect of a quiet festive season, but conscious of Pamela's seething discontent, I shook my head and sighed sympathetically as I passed through the lounge on my way to the classroom to await my students.

I had foreseen that Francisco's non-working, pipe-dreaming life was due to come to an end, so his feeble knock on the door at nine minutes past seven, followed by a piteous trudge across the room to his seat, came as no surprise to me or, I suspect, to the other students. Having just begun to introduce my new 'Butcher's Implements' flashcards; created, I must confess, in order to enable me to interact more fluently with the 'matarife' (according to the dictionary: slaughterman, butcher or knacker - let us say 'pig butcher') on Sunday, I lay my 'six inch beef skinner' card down on the table and asked him to inform us of the cause of his latest woes.

"My mummy say me to get job quick or I go to live with

Uncle Plácido in Madrid. I don't know if there is Line Dancing there." Momentarily stunned by his correct sentence, I went on to invite him to elaborate on his dilemma, and it transpired that his lawyer uncle was anything but placid and would exploit him by making him work for next to nothing at his office, besides frowning upon his line dancing practice which was already driving his mother to distraction. "So I look for job here," he went on, "that I not have to work Tuesday morning."

I promised him that we would all don our 'gorras de pensar' (thinking caps) - allowing my gaze to settle on Alfredo, who quickly stooped to adjust his shoelace - before resuming our butchery vocabulary. After Jorge had struggled manfully to say 'five inch narrow boning knife', Lola, seemingly intent on imperilling her provisional place in the class, once again protested about the obscure nature of the material, even adding that although a 'cuchillo deshuesador estrecho' may well exist, she thought expressing its length in inches to be, and I quote, ludicrous. This time my pursed lips, pensive nodding and baleful stare did not have their usual petrifying effect, so I agreed that we could drop the inches, before brandishing the 'twenty-five inch bone saw' card and begging her to be so kind as to give me a metric translation. As she had only the vaguest idea of how long an inch was, she described a weapon worthy of a Moorish king, which I then pretended to use to hack off her head, much to the amusement of everybody except her. My victory, however, was somewhat diminished by her staying behind and requesting a word in my ear. "I think," she said, "that I shall wait for you to establish an advanced conversation group before I return to class. I find these bizarre cards rather... wearisome, and would prefer just to chat about topical subjects."

After a single glass of almond liqueur I was able to laugh off this minor disappointment, before asking Paco if he had been invited to the 'bautizo y matanza' on Sunday. He said that he had, but that he and Laura would be attending the church service as he had no intention of getting up early and bloodying his hands on his only day of rest. On asking me if I had been to the church yet, I said that apart from popping my head around the door to 'echar un vistazo' (take a peek), I had not, and that being a Church of England Protestant I had assumed that I would not be welcome. Paco laughed and said that the 'cura' (priest), who covered two more villages besides La Puebla, was a friendly old fellow and if I went along to mass one day he would not mind if I gave the wine and wafer a miss. That being the case, I said that I might well attend a service at Christmas - preferably a cheerful one - with the intention of proving to the villagers that I am not a heathen, before adding that I was counting on him to accompany me and tell me what to do. After mumbling his assent - for the village men are not great churchgoers - we sang and hummed along to a selection of country music, before taking our leave 'hasta el domingo'.

Pamela was hissing down the telephone when I went downstairs after the class, and several more mysterious calls were made or received this morning, which, while a welcome respite from her smouldering presence, should have alerted me that trouble was brewing. During lunch and with the noble intention of assuaging her sorrows, I told her that Gerald had solemnly promised to telephone on the two key festive dates and that he and Lena would be coming to stay in January. I will reproduce the rest of our conversation below so that the future reader may witness the cruel way in which my wife broke her unwelcome news to me.

"Oh, I'm afraid we'll miss those calls," she answered.

"Why, my dear? Will we be out?"

"Hmm, we may well be out, but that's irrelevant."

"Ah, yes. I forgot about your mobile device."

"Oh, I shan't be taking that."

"Taking it where, dear?"

"To England. We are going to spend Christmas and the New Year in England. I've booked the outward flight, so there's no point arguing."

(Stunned silence.)

When I recovered my senses, I implored her to put off the trip until the warmer weather as I was so looking forward to the festivities here, apart from the revolting 'turrón' which one is obliged to eat at the end of each meal. She countered this by saying that we would hopefully enjoy many more Christmases in Spain, but that Auntie Cissy, Auntie Lizzie, and a couple more family dinosaurs - my definition, not Pamela's - would not be around forever and would be delighted to see us. "We could even go up north to stay with Uncle Harold," she added maliciously, "and see how his bonsais are coming along." "Bugger Uncle Harold and bugger his stupid bonsais!" I muttered - my rare use of vulgar speech illustrating the depth of my disenchantment - before calling Sancho and taking him for an impromptu walk, during which I delighted him by the frequency and ferocity of my stick throwing.

As I write this, and after a final futile request to be allowed to stay here while she bellows at deaf relatives and plunges through bonsai jungles, my mood is low, while Pamela's has improved perceptibly since she delivered her little 'coup d'état'. I shall have to make the most of Sunday's doubly interesting get-together and put the horrors of overheated sitting rooms and cold muffins out of my head. We are to depart on the 23rd, but the date of our return has yet to be set and will depend, my heartless spouse says, on my behaviour over Christmas. It is but a tiny consolation that we shall be enjoying the warmth of other people's central heating.

Domingo, 14 de Diciembre

Today has been a memorable, if slightly disturbing, day which has increased my knowledge of Spanish customs and may well hasten my conversion to vegetarianism. An unaccustomed evening nap has enabled me to shake off the slight stupor caused by much feasting and more than adequate drinking, so I shall set down the events of the day while they are still fresh in my mind.

Fresh, indeed, like the blood spurting out of the pig's neck this morning, which is by no means the best way to enjoy a sunrise, especially when preceded by the pinning of the terrified brute to the butcher's slab; in this case a sturdy table. The next time that somebody refers to a person or animal as squealing like a pig, I shall be forced to correct them - unless it is, in fact, another pig - because the squeals of today's ex-pig were uniquely distressing and are still, if the reader will pardon my rare use of a cliché, echoing in my ears.

When I arrived at the finca just before sunrise, several middle-aged and elderly men were seated around a small bonfire and already tucking into a hearty breakfast, among them Ana's father and his aged friend Feliciano, the chief 'matarife'. Having already eaten my toast and cornflakes, I declined their offer of a blood sausage sandwich, but did partake of a small glass of 'aguardiente' which, despite burning my throat and sending jets of steam from my nostrils, certainly warmed me up. After another glass we all made for the pig enclosure where two of the younger men - of about my age - cornered the condemned pig, before Feliciano stuck a large metal hook under its jaw and they led the unhappy creature back to the table. It was at this point that the serious squealing began, as the beast was lifted onto the table and ropes tied around its legs to secure it there, before it reached a crescendo when the matarife jabbed a knife skilfully into its neck while an assistant held a bucket to catch the copious blood which came pouring out. The blood, I was told, would be used to make 'morcilla' sausages like the ones they had just scoffed.

The squealing over, I helped myself to another small glass of aguardiente to calm my rattled nerves, before a blowtorch was produced to burn the hair unceremoniously from the corpse. After it had been dowsed with hot water, I was requested to help to scrub it clean, so I positioned myself behind the body in order not to see its poor little piggy eyes, and within twenty minutes we had polished him as white and almost as smooth as a baby's bottom. After we had positioned the pig belly up, the matarife produced a formidable knife and sliced the body open along its entire length, before delving inside to cut out the organs.

At this point, Andy appeared in his Sunday best and asked me if I was enjoying the show so far. I took advantage of his presence to turn my back on the table and thus avoid witnessing the plundering of the pig's insides, before telling him that I was finding it all fascinating. "Yes," he said, "I can see your hand shaking with excitement. Let's have a little snifter of this foul firewater." While drinking his first and my fourth glass of aguardiente, Andy told his father-in-law, who had a bundle of intestines in his hands, that it was time for him to get ready to go to church, so he dropped the 'tripas' into a bucket and reluctantly shuffled away to scrub himself up and put on 'ese maldito traje y la jodida corbata' (that damned suit and f***ing tie) - a true rustic if ever I saw one.

By this time several women had approached to carry the blood and innards off to the kitchen - hired hands, Feliciano explained, as the ladies of the family would never miss a good baptism - before the carcass was splayed open and he cut off the head and handed it to me. Transporting this heavy, bloodied burden to the kitchen was possibly the single most disagreeable task of the day, but I now console myself with the thought that it was an experience that the vast majority of expats are unlikely to have. The fact that Ana - looking lovely in a body-hugging green dress - took a photograph of me, though annoying at the time, has at least immortalised this daring feat, although I very much doubt that I shall use it on the cover of the published journals.

When I returned to our outdoor abattoir, Feliciano had carved off the legs and begun to slice out the fat in order to get to the ribs, which he then skilfully extracted before cutting out what were to become our lunchtime chops. After much toing and froing, the centre of operations was relocated to the kitchen, where the women were preparing the seasonings amid boiling pans and several devices which looked like instruments of torture, but were in fact mincers and sausage makers. With most of the manly work done, I sat down for a rest and drank a final tot of aguardiente, before returning to the kitchen to watch the amazing process of converting almost every part of an animal which only two hours ago had been snuffling round without a care in the world into edible matter. Only the nauseating stench of the intestines being emptied, prior to becoming sausage skins, drove me out into the fresh air, before I scrubbed my hands and arms thoroughly and changed into my smarter clothes.

At about half past twelve the cars began to arrive from the village and when I spotted Pamela arriving with Paco and Laura, I approached them and told them all about my stimulating morning, including my transportation of the head to the kitchen. Pamela was impressed by this feat until Andy, who had sneaked up behind me, told her that I'd turned as green as a gooseberry when they 'cut the fecker open'. "I see you've acquired a little Dutch courage since then," she said, smelling my breath, "but you might need another drink when you see the surprise guest." She would not disclose who this person was, but when Nerys drew up in her little car my worst fear was realised, as it was none other than Uncle Harold, who had soon levered his pedantic bulk from the vehicle.

Seeing me turn red and grimace, my wife said that I need not fear, because he was staying with Nerys and that they were setting off on holiday to Lanzarote the next day. "But Pamela," I spluttered, "the back of the car is full of bonsais!" We had hoped to rid ourselves of another dozen of the stunted little objects at the lunch, but Pamela told me not to worry. "Ernest!" boomed that very man into my left earhole, "good to see you! Nerys and I are now an item, as you can see. What do you think of that?" I thought it a blessing for the rest of humanity, but said that I was delighted and that I had always seen them as being very compatible, before I asked him if she would be moving to England.

"Not on your life, old chap," he said, "it's Spain all the way for my Welsh gal and me. I'm looking to buy a pad near your village."

"But what about your bonsais?" I asked.

"Oh, stuff the bonsais. That was just the craze of a loveless man. Stupid little things anyway, but I can have the lot of them sent over if you'd like them."

After graciously declining his offer, we made our way into the dining room, where I kissed Ana on both cheeks, gave her a brotherly hug, and patted the baby on the head. There were a great variety of dishes, which I thought an astonishing accomplishment until Andy told me that yet more hired help had brought most of them ready prepared, except for the chops, which were indeed those that had been hacked out of this morning's victim, and one more delicacy called 'criadillas' which the 'pig ladies' had prepared especially as it was, he said, typical baptism fare. He urged me to try this meaty and oniony dish, which I did, before he made the mistake of saying, "It's made of the pig's bollocks." Made the mistake, I say, because it was upon his silk shirt and tie that it landed when it came spurting out of my mouth, so I rather think that the joke was on him in the end. Criadillas are delicious if you don't know what they are, but from now on every time I eat something proceeding from a pig, I will hear the awful squealing, so, rather than eating ruinously expensive lamb or beef, or Ernestina, I shall officially become a vegetarian from the first day of Gerald and Lena's next visit.

We all spent an enjoyable afternoon and I spoke to most of the people present, revelling in my mastery of the language which the wine appeared to augment and steering clear of Nerys and Harold, from whose name I feel I can drop the Uncle now that she has adopted him. At leave-taking time I was finally compelled to address them, so I asked them how long they were going to Lanzarote for. "Just a week, old man," he said, "and back to Wales for Christmas before the four of us meet up at mine to celebrate the New Year."

The enthusiasm I mustered to record the day's news has once again deserted me on writing that final sentence, which in itself feels like a sentence - up to two weeks deprived of my home, my plot, my friends, my animals and Sancho. Tomorrow I shall take the ten bonsai trees which remain in the car to the village square with a note inviting the villagers to take one. Perhaps they will help to keep my memory alive while I am in exile.

Jueves, 18 de Diciembre

Not until last night's successful class and post-class tête-à-tête with Paco did my spirits begin to rise after Sunday's news of the deplorable arrangements that Pamela had made behind my back. The absence of clever clogs Lola and the fact that Francisco has secured a part-time job in a supermarket made it the most pleasant lesson for several weeks and we even managed to converse for twenty minutes at the end of the class without causing me to fall upon the almond liqueur bottle to calm my nerves.

Marta and Jorge told the rest of us about their plans for the festive season, which almost made me weep with envy, so cosy, traditional and Spanish were their scheduled activities, before Paco told us that he and Laura would be visiting her elderly aunt in Almansa, proving beyond reasonable doubt that she really does exist. Alfredo, visibly relieved by no longer being silently pressured into creating a job for our potty companion, said that he would be spending Christmas in Leicester with Marjorie's family and looked forward to practising his English, singing carols, and pulling crackers. The fact that the thought of going to England did not fill him with despondency made me feel a little more cheerful, as did Francisco's account of his first days in his new job.

"It's a happy job," he said, "and lot of moving. I work on cajero (till) and laugh with customers, then I dance down pasillo (aisle) to fill estantes (shelves) and laugh with compañeros. Everybody laugh lot with me and I am free for Line Dancing Tuesdays. Better than stupid desk and pervertido boss and very bored compañeros."

So much happiness is contagious and we parted with much well-wishing and my firm avowal to be back for our next class on the 8th of January, by which date Pamela has promised that we will be here, although I shall of course press for an earlier return in order to celebrate 'The Day of the Kings' on Spanish soil. I now feel slightly less like a man on death row and must begin to make preparations for the care of my animals in my absence.

Viernes 19 de Diciembre

The man who I hope to entrust with the care of my animals walked through the house this morning while I was weeding my plot, leaving a dense cloud of cachimba smoke in his wake.

Quick thinking as always, I told him that the Moors considered it bad for the health to smoke the pipe whilst in motion, at which he simply shrugged, before I went on to say that it also attracted evil spirits, upon which he took the top off and threw the little coal onto my plot, where it lay smouldering among the turnips, much to Sancho's perplexity. Superstition is still rife among the old folk here, I am happy to say.

While we were facing my thriving plot - for we are yet to suffer a single freezing night despite now being prepared for Arctic temperatures - I asked him when my crops would be ready to collect. After he had assured me that everything would be safe in the ground until January, I asked him if he would be able to look after my livestock for up to two weeks over the Christmas period. He had already said that he would be delighted and that they would also be happy to take Sancho in until we returned, before I realised that he was actually *speaking* to me, rather than miming - progress indeed! I thanked him gratefully for his promise of assistance, but said that Sancho's arrangements had already been made, which they hadn't, but I have no wish to return to find him suffering from nicotine as well as stick addiction. While I trust Nora and Angeles implicitly, one cannot forget their advanced age, so I rang Paco to ask him to look in now and again. While I was at the phone I also rang Andy, Alfredo and Trevor, who all promised to drop by when they could, so in the case of serious illness or death, my animals should still get fed.

I was about to call on Rocío and Pedro to inform them of our impending absence, when I remembered my burning desire to buy their plot, so, after Pamela had confirmed that I had €6000 to bargain with - the least she could do after ruining my Christmas - I strode round and knocked on their door with the intention of sealing the deal there and then. Rocío welcomed me into their sitting room where Pedro was playing his guitar within a cloud of smoke - thank goodness he doesn't possess a cachimba - and I told her that we were going away for up to a fortnight. She promised that they would pop their heads over the fence to check that all was well and it was at this point that I decided to make my final offer. I told Rocío that one million pesetas was as high as Pamela would allow me to go, hoping that this intimation that my wife held the purse strings would appeal to her womanly pride, and she asked me how much that was in euros. When I told her, though I am sure that she knew, she said that it didn't sound very much for a fine piece of village land, but that she would think about it and let me know soon. This I took to mean yes in gypsy language and her final acceptance of the offer will enable me to mentally plan my new domain while listening to the English rain beating on the windows, if that noise is not drowned out by the dratted television which I expect to be omnipresent in every household we visit. After declining my offer of another half dozen bonsai trees, I took my leave with a pointed 'hasta pronto' (see you soon) as I fully expect her to call round very pronto to accept my generous offer.

Sábado, 20 de Diciembre

A sunny but very chilly morning saw Alfredo reassert his marginal golfing superiority and win today's game by four shots. Ever the graceful loser, I complemented him on his game - always strong in dry conditions - and felt that I did not deserve the depressing news that he then gave me over our beer and mixed nuts. To be fair to Alfredo, he did first ask me if I really wanted to know the exact details of the house transaction and I said that I most certainly did. The exact details, he had discovered, were that the forty thousand euros which we had paid in cash had gone into the agent's pocket, or briefcase, and stayed there. "You mean he kept it all?" I blurted out, momentarily forgetting that Spanish is now my number one language, to which he replied that as the former owner had simply told the agent how much he wanted for the property, the agent, seeing how keen I was, had simply pushed up the price and kept the difference. This, he said, was common practice, but it was a pity that I had not made enquiries and sought out the owner, as I could have saved myself all that money.

On the drive back I only spoke once, to beg Alfredo never to mention this catastrophe to Pamela, or even to his wife Marjorie, and he assured me that he was a 'tumba', or tomb, meaning, I hoped, that he wouldn't. I reflected that a shameless robbery of this description could never happen in the strictly regulated housing market of my native country, but that did not make the thought of our coming visit any more appealing. By the time he dropped me off outside Integración I had partially assimilated this calamity and entered the house with an especially cheery greeting. "What's wrong?" replied my hyper-perceptive wife. "Oh, Alfredo thrashed me," I said, which seemed to do the trick. She must *never* know.

Domingo, 21 de Diciembre

Still feeling low after yesterday's news - a mood exacerbated by our imminent departure and the fact that Rocío has yet to call round to accept my offer - I shall make what may well be my last journal entry of the year, as I cannot imagine that anything noteworthy will happen on our trip. Pamela has already started packing and is looking forward to the change of scene, but I have yet to dig out my woollies. She has also bought sundry presents for her relatives, Marcus, Harold and one or two other people, and has bought a few extra gifts in case I wish to look up any of my long lost relatives or see my old friends at the golf club. I doubt that I shall bother to visit the club, as to boast about my enviable lifestyle in Spain is not in my nature, especially when most of the poor chaps will still be packing themselves like sardines into the train to London every day.

All that remains now is to pack, take Sancho to Andy's, and leave everything in order for Nora's stewardship. If Rocío accepts my offer before we leave, so much the better, but with my current luck, I doubt that she will.

Lunes, 22 de Diciembre

Rocío called round this morning to accept my offer of €6000, which she would like in cash, but this splendid news soon paled into insignificance when Gerald telephoned to tell us that Lena is expecting a baby. This news was initially transmitted to me through Pamela's whoops of joy which brought me scurrying in from the plot to find out what had happened. It transpires that Lena is two months 'gone', which means that it is certainly Gerald's, although I never doubted the relative chastity of the angelic mother-to-be. This proves my fears regarding my son's possible impotency to be unfounded and it is quite possible that the baby was conceived here at about the time of Pamela's birthday, but I decided that it was not the time to question Gerald about their mating history.

After lengthy congratulations from each of us to each of them, Pamela finally hung up the phone and went to fetch a bottle of cava from the fridge. I was just as overjoyed as my wife by the glad tidings, for this now cements their relationship and lays the foundations for the Postlethwaite - or even Postlethwaite-Krankl - dynasty which in generations to come will be well-respected in this part of Spain, but I did point out that they are not yet married. Knowing the Germans to be an essentially conservative race, I suggested that we fly to Germany right away in order to assist the Krankl's with the wedding preparations which would undoubtedly already be underway. Pamela laughed, called me an old fuddy-duddy, and said that from what she had ascertained, Lena's mother and father were just as liberal as she was and would not expect them to get married just because a baby was on the way.

Not wishing to diminish Pamela's happiness by assuring her that at some point in the next seven months they will be tying the knot, or my name is not Ernesto Postlethwaite, we clinked glasses and toasted the happy couple and our first grandchild, who will one day come to inhabit a much expanded Integración.

2009 promises to be a very splendid year indeed!

To be continued…

arlowe.barrybraithwaite@gmail.com

4332874R00097

Printed in Germany
by Amazon Distribution
GmbH, Leipzig